Mango Shake

edited by
Debjani Chatterjee

Tindal
Street
Press

First published in July 2006 by
Tindal Street Press Ltd.
217 The Custard Factory, Gibb Street, Birmingham B9 4AA
www.tindalstreet.co.uk

ISBN 0 9547913 6 3
EAN 978 0 9547913 6 0

Typeset by Country Setting, Kingsdown, Kent.
Printed and bound in Great Britain by Clays Ltd, St Ives PLC

Mango Shake

Contents

Introduction

A good anthology is like a tasty kedgeree – or *khichuri* as we say in Bengali. It should have a choice mix of fresh and spicy ingredients; a colour, texture and flavour that command attention; and a delicious and substantial content that hits the right spot in the reader. It could also be described as a fruit cocktail or a stir-fry. This is what I had in mind when sifting through a range of short fiction by regional writers, but I was looking also for a quality that would make each stand out from the crowd – the resulting dish is the eight striking stories in *Mango Shake* that indicate such potential and talent.

Like a good poem, a short story quickly draws in the reader and has an impact that lingers in the mind. Like a good poem too, it repays more than one reading. The stories in *Mango Shake* will tempt the reader to revisit them – and to look out for future work from these writers. There are exciting stories rooted in modern-day urban culture from three young British men with South Asian ethnicity. There are also lyrical tales of myth and magic by a British woman with a Guyanese background, tales that transport us to the warm beaches of her homeland.

This showcase anthology presents two stories by each of four talented writers from mid-England whose work enriches the contemporary landscape of the English short story with their own distinctive charm, sparkle and diversity. The four writers are first- or second-generation immigrants in Britain, but anyone expecting homogeneity in their writing would be very mistaken – each story is uniquely different – the variety of style and subject matter is no small part of *Mango Shake*'s attraction.

Zorina Ishmail-Bibby's 'Ole Man's Luck' is a timeless, dreamlike tale of a little girl who encounters a strange old fisherman in a landscape where sunlight 'gleams through patchworks of mango and oleander leaves' and red hibiscus flowers float on the waters that wash between the shores of South America and the Caribbean. 'Miss Gusta's Lil' School' is a sensitive study of innocence and hypocrisy. Inspired by her own childhood, Ishmail-Bibby weaves rich and colourful tapestries.

Anish Desai's stories question family responsibilities and loyalties. 'Brimful of Hope' builds a tense atmosphere in which characters oscillate between hope and despair. Living secretly in his parents' empty house, Manu is desperate to remember the familiar words of the *Gayatri* mantra; he feels trapped as the birth of his new baby coincides with his father's death and his mother's return to India. In Desai's imaginative 'Busy Minds Are Blind', a lonely little boy, neglected by his parents, tries to stay out of sight. When his grandmother takes him on a visit to the zoo, he is strangely drawn to what seems an empty cage.

Bobby Nayyar's engaging stories of work and sex are set in an inner-city Birmingham that is presented with gritty authenticity. In 'The Syndicate of Tears' seven immigrant women work on an assembly-line in a clothing factory in a run-down area, but dream of winning the lottery jackpot. Events take a dramatic turn when one of them realizes her dream. Nayyar's 'Handsworth Songs' has a fast-paced monologue style that is very different in tone. The narrator reflects on the identities that others thrust on him:

> *When you travel they see a Muslim, when you eat they*
> *see a Hindu, when you grow a beard they see a Sikh*
> *. . . The problem of race becomes clearer when you*
> *go to secondary school. Everybody hates everybody.*

Harpreet Singh's 'Earth Versus Spider' presents an intriguing idea in a witty 'twist-in-the-tale' narrative. In the hilarious 'Simran Kaur in Great Barr', Aunty Neeta, 'an amazing Birmingham woman', becomes a bus driver, TV celebrity and role model, proving that she has 'the strong arms to turn the wheel'. Her success upsets her 'big sulking donkey' of a husband and he decides to assert himself by organizing the most impressive display of Diwali fireworks. The dynamics of family life are at the heart of this and most of *Mango Shake*'s other stories.

Many of the tales also delight with their sharply observed portrayals of childhood. The insightful eponymous narrator of 'Simran Kaur in Great Barr' is a Brummie schoolgirl on the brink of discovering her vocation as a writer. Singh reserves the last word for Simran:

> *Then I sensed patterns of life spreading out and con-*
> *necting somewhere on the periphery, just out of sight.*
> *I could appreciate their chatter and movement, taking*
> *shape slowly, speaking in strange accents. I closed*
> *my eyes and waited for something to begin. I saw*
> *them line up to tell me their tales, in confidence and*
> *with care, just for me and my family.*

The reader will recognize that these inspired words are prophetic, too, of British South Asian writing as a whole.

Debjani Chatterjee
May 2006

Zorina Ishmail-Bibby

ZORINA ISHMAIL-BIBBY is originally from Guyana and moved to Britain in the 1960s. Her short stories have been broadcast on the World Service and on BBC Radio 4. A poetry collection, *After a Cold Season Rising*, was published in 1988. Zorina has worked for many years in adult education teaching ESOL, with articles published on this subject. At present she continues to write, paint and facilitate the Chameleon Writers Group in Northamptonshire.

Ole Man's Luck

Zorina Ishmail-Bibby

Zohra only became reconciled to the new house slowly. It was too open and light. The Muranese glass windows with their deeply etched surfaces let in and distorted sunlight. They imprisoned her in their brittle embrace, blocking out life outside. There were none of the dark corners found in Capa's house where she could hide.

She had recently met Ole Man, who took care of their backyard. She could see his house from the kitchen window. Often he sat enmeshed in seines as he mended them on his veranda.

Ole Man always so quiet, she thought. All he do is smoke cigarette and look at people.

At nightfall, after a long day's fishing, he would pluck the strings of his sitar. The sound rose discordantly through the Muranese glass windows, combining the softness of the river and the throbbing of the wind.

On moonlit nights, Zohra liked to watch them hauling home their catch of gallibaca or snook. Then the fish lay on his veranda, shimmering in silver scales.

One day, as she drew water from the standpipe outside Ole Man's house, he lay in his hammock staring at the shadowy patterns made by the oleander leaves.

'Howdy,' she said. 'You catch any fish today?'

'Not much.'

'What happen, Ole Man?'

'Sometimes it's like that.'

Her bucket overflowed, and she turned off the tap.

'It depend on luck, you know,' he added quietly.

'Luck?'

'If you don't have luck in this business, you done for.'

'But you always catch plenty fish.'

'Not always.' He shook his white head.

'But everybody say you is the best fisherman on the Corentyne.'

'One day, one day, *Gonga te*.'

'What?'

'Maybe me luck will run out.'

'That can't happen.'

'Maybe Water Mama won't like me no more.'

'Eh? Who is Water Mama?'

'She does give fisherman luck.'

'Oh. Me don't know she.'

'If she want, she could curse we so we not get any fish.'

Zohra had heard of Old Hags and Jumbees, but not of Water Mama. The thought made her nervous. The river suddenly seemed like a strange place.

'Me hope you get some fish soon,' she said politely, as she picked up her bucket.

'We will see.'

After this conversation Zohra took a keen interest in Ole Man. Each day she would ask, 'Ole Man catch any fish?'

'Why you ask?' Gramma enquired.

'Nothin'.'

'That is five times that you ask this week!'

'He catch any today?'

'Yes, yes! When Ole Man does never catch fish?'

Zohra shrugged. She felt Ole Man had entrusted her with a special piece of information, so she said nothing more.

A few weeks later, Zohra went for a walk on the sea wall. The river stretched taut, sombrely projecting isolated fishing boats. Something vertical stood on the deck of a red one.

Is a man or a mast? Zohra wondered, shading her eyes. Then it moved.

Oh, is a man wearin' a white singlet, she thought. That must be Ole Man on *Sea Lion*. He throw somethin' in the river.

Impelled by curiosity, Zohra ran down the sea wall and waded into the water. She could see Ole Man quite clearly now. His eyes were closed. What floatin' on the water? Zohra wondered. She looked carefully. 'Red hibiscus!' she whispered.

At this point, Ole Man opened his eyes and looked about him. Then his eyes came to rest on her. It made Zohra feel strange. She began to turn away.

'Where you goin'?' Ole Man called.

'Home,' she said, then asked hesitantly, 'You catch any fish today?'

'No luck.'

'Oh!'

'But maybe Water Mama will hear me.'

'Why?'

'I just do *pooja*.'

Zohra waited as Ole Man swung himself from the boat and waded through the scattered flower offerings. He stopped before the small girl and looked down on her.

'You got good luck,' he announced.

'Wha-at?'

'Your luck newborn.'

'Me don't know what you mean.'

'Give me your luck.'

'But –'

'Water Mama can't refuse that. Your luck fresh like them hibiscus flower. Give me your luck.'

Zohra stared at his pleading face, unsure of how to respond.

'But me can't give you anythin'. Ask Gramma.'

'Please say you will give me your luck.'

Ole Man's intensity and urgency alarmed her.

'Me goin', Ole Man,' Zohra cried and ran out of the water as quickly as she could.

'Wait! Don't go way!'

But the child ran faster still until she gained the sea wall. Then, for a moment, she looked around. Ole Man was just another vertical line in the glass of the river. He no longer looked threatening. Yet she ran on, feeling as though the world had turned to Muranese glass and Ole Man was the biggest splinter of frightening light.

Zohra didn't visit the beach for some time after this in case she met Ole Man. Once she tiptoed past him as he sat on his empty fish-cart.

'Ole Man got any fish today, Aunty?' Zohra asked her aunt when she returned home.

'No. Things bad with poor Ole Man. He ain't been too well.'

Though Zohra avoided Ole Man physically, she became obsessed by his sad face and strange request. After her evening meal, she would sit quietly behind the kitchen window to listen to his sitar.

The thing cryin', she reflected.

The sound splintered her mind like slow-moving spikes of light. Yet she felt compelled to listen. One evening, Ole Man did not play. Zohra worried about it.

'What wrong with Ole Man?'

'He ain't feelin' well,' Gramma said. 'His daughter say is the first time he sick in years.'

Zohra couldn't sleep all night. Next day, she made an excuse to go into the backyard so that she could see Ole Man. Me will pass his veranda, she thought. Me won't worry him.

As she passed Ole Man's veranda, she heard the ropes of his hammock creak. Ole Man lay asleep in his hammock, wrapped in his seine. His beard so long, Zohra thought. And why he rocking about so much in the hammock?

Zohra crouched back in the shade of the oleander tree as Ole Man heaved himself out of the hammock and looked around wildly. He tore the seine away from his body and threw it towards Zohra. 'They catchin' me! They catchin' me!' he cried.

As Ole Man tried to fight off his unseen attackers, his energy was so great that it electrified the child. He stood panting, seeming to look right through Zohra. Again she felt the splinters penetrating her. Then his energy ebbed, and he noticed her. 'Oh, is only you!' he whispered. 'Me just had a bad dream.'

Zohra could not reply.

'Me dream Water Mama catchin' me in seine. Man, was so real!'

'You sick?' Zohra asked, trembling.

'Me luck gone. Me won't catch no more fish.'

'Sorry you sick.'

Ole Man waved a tired arm at her.

'Zohra! Zohra!' Gramma called from the kitchen window. 'Is nearly school time.'

Zohra seized this summons as an excuse to escape. Upstairs, Gramma looked at her rather sternly. 'Why you disturb Ole Man? You know he ain't well.'

'Me didn't do nothin'.'

'The doctor comin' to see him.'

'He sick bad?'

'Yes, but he won't go to hospital.'

Now Zohra knew that Ole Man was seriously ill. Everyone went to the dispenser or pharmacist for ordinary illnesses. The hospital meant that Ole Man was very ill indeed. She worried all day about him, and never saw the words on the blackboard at school. Instead Ole Man rose before her, wrestling with the seine. He did look like a dead man, wrap up in it, Zohra thought. Then, frightened at the idea of death, she consoled herself: But he can't die. He is the best fisherman on the Corentyne.

After school, she asked Gramma some more about him.

'He really sick,' Gramma said. 'Your aunty going to take some special broth for him.'

'Me want to go.'

'Well, ask Aunty.'

After much persuading, Zohra went with her aunt. Ole Man's daughter sat by the hammock, wiping the sweat from his face.

'How he doin'?' Zohra's aunt asked.

'Bad. The doctor say he got weak heart. Me wish he would go to hospital,' the daughter said.

'Why he ain't goin'?'

Ole Man suddenly sat up. 'Me can't go. Tell them not to take me, missis.'

'But why?'

'Me can't leave the river.'

'You ain't realize how bad you sick, Ole Man?'

'Hospital can't help me, only a sign from . . .' He sank back, murmuring.

'What he say?' asked Zohra's aunt.

'Oh, Miss Fisul, he say "Water Mama". Me really frighten.

He never stop talkin' bout Water Mama all the time.' Ole Man's daughter looked anxious.

'Don't worry,' Zohra's aunt comforted. 'If he take things easy, he should be okay.' Then she added softly, almost to herself, 'But is almost like he gettin' out his head.'

Zohra shuddered. 'Ole Man ain't mad,' she said quietly.

'What you know bout madness, chile?' her aunt asked.

Zohra thought of Ole Man and his red flower offerings. 'He ain't mad,' she kept repeating to herself.

She moved away from the veranda and stood under the oleander tree. Maybe if me could give him back his luck, she thought, then he might get better. Tomorrow I will do it.

That night, Zohra slept more deeply than she had done for weeks, until a hammering on the back door awakened her. Her aunt ran to see what was happening. Zohra and other members of the family followed.

Ole Man's daughter stood in the fading moonlight. Her beautiful black hair swathed her in mourning as she wept. 'Pa run way to sea wall, Miss Fisul. He just jump outta the hammock and say he goin' to *Sea Lion*.'

'You call Mr Ferguson to help?'

'He ain't answerin'.'

'Wait, I comin'.' Aunty ran to the bedroom, threw on some clothes and told Gramma to send Mr Ferguson down to the beach. Then she disappeared down the back steps with Ole Man's daughter.

'Go back to you bed,' Gramma told Zohra.

'Me can't.'

Gramma sighed, then nodded. 'Well, sit down and wrap up in a blanket then.'

So Zohra sat in the big Morris chair, smothered in a blanket. She saw Ole Man again; his bloodshot eyes pleaded with her. The child shrank back. Then she thought she heard the sitar sobbing. But outside her, all remained quiet for a time.

A weeping first broke the stillness. The family rushed to the kitchen window. In the last vestiges of moonlight, they saw Mr Ferguson bearing Ole Man in his arms. The fisherman's white singlet gleamed through patchworks of mango and oleander leaves. It looked like the scales of fish that Ole Man himself had once hauled into the yard.

'He dead! He dead!' wailed the daughter.

'Oh, my God!' said Gramma. Then, remembering Zohra, she said, 'Go inside, baby.'

'No, Gramma.'

'Go on.'

But Zohra clung to the windowsill, staring at the dead fisherman's body.

'What happen?' Gramma asked at length.

'He just lyin' like this on *Sea Lion*,' the daughter sobbed. 'He had blood on his head and them hibiscus flowers in his hand.'

Zohra began to shiver. 'Go in,' her grandmother urged.

'No, no,' the child whispered. He don't need me luck now. It too late, she thought.

A great sadness fell upon her. It surrounded her as completely as the Muranese glass world, cutting into her heart and sobbing wildly like Ole Man's sitar.

Miss Gusta's Lil' School
Zorina Ishmail-Bibby

Capa's house looked on to the main road of the village. Each day she watched the *bara* lady selling her crunchy *bara* and chutney to cinema-goers. She saw Mrs Kalamadin squabbling with people in the shop, and their grey donkey returning from the wharf, laden with sugar sacks. But none of these interested her as much as Miss Gusta did. Zohra had admired the lady long before personal contact and the smell of guavas ripened their acquaintance into friendship.

Miss Gusta passed Capa's house every Sunday on the way to church, flanked on either side by a sister. The two Misses Braithwaite seemed to protect their younger sister from the onslaught of vulgar eyes as they walked along the road. Miss Joycelyn's nearsighted squint discouraged people. So did Miss Esther's dignity as she rose above her two sisters, surveying the world with awesome detachment. Miss Gusta walked, sheltered between them. 'Oh, Miss Gusta look so nice in her crinoline hat and her stockings shining like dew!' Zohra would say in wonder.

Each Sunday at eight o'clock Zohra anxiously awaited Miss Gusta by the front window. 'They coming!' her voice rang out each week, sure as a gospel singer. 'I can see their lace dress by the sweetie tree!'

The Misses Braithwaite dressed alike. The older sisters wore their clothes grimly like a challenge – a glove flung in the face of the world. Miss Gusta tried to follow suit, but femininity permeated her clothes in the way she wore her belt or pinned the flowers on her hat. Even at middle age, her eyes showed a girlish vulnerability that her sisters appeared to foster and guard. Early in their acquaintance, this expression had appealed to Zohra's imagination, long before she succumbed to the luscious guava scent that surrounded Miss Gusta.

One Sunday Zohra spoke to them as they passed by. 'Mornin', Miss Gusta!' she cried as the sisters neared Capa's house.

They paused to look, standing before Uncle Mus's shop. 'Eh, eh!' Miss Gusta answered. 'You grow big, chile. You don't think so, Sis Joycie?' She turned to her sisters, pleading for agreement. 'What you say, Sis Essie?'

Her two sisters nodded. 'The chile growin',' Miss Joycelyn agreed.

'Say howdy to Gramma for us,' Miss Essie said.

'Thanks,' Zohra replied, overburdened with this honour. Then she spent the rest of the day happily telling everyone about the sisters.

So when Zohra heard that she was going to attend Miss Gusta's kindergarten, she awaited her first day impatiently. 'Me going to Miss Gusta's school,' she boasted to her friends in Long Range Yard. 'Every day I will see her crinoline hat and lace dress.'

But Zohra was disappointed. Miss Gusta wore a stiffly starched cotton dress and her hair neatly tied back in plaits. 'Oh Miss Gusta,' Zohra exclaimed when she arrived at the school. 'What happen to all you nice clothes and stockings?'

Miss Gusta looked startled. 'But that's me church clothes, chile.'

'Why you only wear them for church?'

'We should only dress up for the Lord. Who else should we dress for?'

'I did think you wear those all the time.'

'No, no, dear. Come on. We calling register now.' Miss Gusta put an arm around Zohra and drew her into the house.

By this time, the ravishing smell of ripe guavas drifted from Miss Gusta to distract Zohra, quenching her desire for that lady's beautiful clothes and silencing further enquiries. Zohra was happy to live in Miss Gusta's guava atmosphere.

At the kindergarten, each sister had a task. Miss Gusta said prayers and taught the children. Miss Joycelyn saw the children do their exercises and inspected their nails, while Miss Esther sat with the naughty ones after school. Each morning the routine followed the same pattern.

'Mawnin chil'ren,' Miss Gusta said.

'Mawnin Miss Gusta.'

'Now let us pray.'

During the first week of school, Zohra prayed: 'Allah bless Mommy, Aunty, Henry, Gramma . . .'

'Our Father which art in heaven,' prayed the class.

'Why Mommy didn't teach me that one?' Zohra wondered.

Each day the question arose in her mind but, as she wished to fit in with the rest of the class, Zohra adopted their version of prayer and pushed aside puzzling questions.

After prayers, Miss Gusta usually told Bible stories. She told her favourite, 'Suffer the little children to come to me', very often. 'Then Jesus say: "Suffer the lil' chil'ren to come to me," but only if you good He will say that to you. Is them chil'ren who say prayer, honour they father and they mother and love they neighbour who He will take to them green pastures in heaven. If you do these things, you will live on honey and manna fo' the rest o' you everlastin' life. Amen.'

This outburst forced Miss Gusta to stop for breath.

Who is Jee-sus? Zohra would think. Only Allah livin' in heaven.

'And the Lawd say you must love everybody, chil'ren,' Miss Gusta would continue. 'Even people you all don't like. Love them, then life not hard fo' you. But Lawd Jesus!' she would say and close her eyes in ecstasy. 'Adore He! Beautiful Jesus dyin' on the cross. Look at His shinin' face and side bleedin', yet He smile and love everybody. Nobody can help lovin' He – we Saviour, we King!'

Her words seldom meant much to the children, but at these times, Miss Gusta radiated love and conquered them. The class sat spellbound, some sucking their fingers, others half-asleep and the rest open-mouthed. Even Zohra's puzzlement about Jesus disappeared in her love for Miss Gusta.

Nor did Miss Gusta swerve domestically from the theme of love and obedience that she preached. Miss Joycie usually grumbled about the children's dirty nails and runny noses. One afternoon she erupted in the middle of an arithmetic lesson: 'Lucille and Chandra, you stayin' in this afternoon. Look at you nails! You too, Frankie. What you mother give you kerchief for? Blow you nose, boy!'

Lucille began to whimper. Miss Gusta's annoyance at this interruption revealed itself in the way her chalk squeaked on the blackboard and in the rapid suppression of a frown. Then a look of sweet mildness spread over her face. 'Awright, sister.'

Once Zohra overheard Miss Essie dryly complaining while she and Frankie were playing bus drivers on the veranda. She stood with her back to the nearby classroom window. 'You know me catch Mickey peepin' at Lucille panties yesterday? It ain't decent. Maybe we should ask them parents to make them wear long dresses.'

'Chil'ren just lil' curious,' Miss Gusta gently explained.

'But we mustn't encourage them to think bad things from that young.'

Zohra heard Miss Gusta sigh. 'You think we should write a letter to them parents and ask that the gals wear long dress?'

There was another pause. Then she said, 'Awright, Sis Essie. You bound to know best; after all, you mind me ever since me lil'. You older and wiser.'

This conversation resulted in a letter to each girl's parents asking them to dress their children in longer clothes. So Miss Gusta's girls came to be nicknamed 'Lil' Mother Sallies' because their long clothes reminded people of Mother Sally in the Christmas masquerades.

Zohra adapted herself to the Misses Braithwaite's school. She enjoyed the distinction of being called 'Lil' Mother Sally'. The nickname made her feel she belonged to Miss Gusta.

As Zohra grew to know her teacher, she also developed an ambivalent attitude towards religion. At school she accepted the Trinity, thinking of Christ as the handsome, romantic hero of a film whom Miss Gusta loved. At home Allah remained the stern, just Being who demanded retribution for naughtiness and answered prayers only if one sacrificed pleasant things.

Zohra found lessons the most interesting change in her life, for Miss Gusta spoke of the alphabet as though it were something deliciously edible. 'A,' said Miss Gusta, 'for a-p-p-le that you eat at Christmas time. And B for . . .? What Gary Sobers does play cricket with?'

'Bat! Bat!' the children shouted.

'Now spell it!'

The class triumphantly spelled the word.

'And C? C-c? Tell we, Claudie.'

'Cat! Is a cat!'

'Yes, just like Tabby. Tabby! Mssh, mssh! Come, show them how you look, Tabby.'

Tabby bounded up, rubbing his head against her legs. Zohra felt a spurt of jealousy. He too must like the guava smell, she thought.

The days fell back like the read pages of an endless book, piling one on the other. Zohra's imagination expanded under Miss Gusta's care. Ordinary objects began to live new lives and, after a while, she incorporated the things she saw in an alphabet of her own. She began to act as Miss Gusta before the wardrobe mirror, wearing her mother's hat as well as an old lace tablecloth around her shoulders.

'A for what, Mickey?' Zohra asked her image, imitating Miss Gusta's voice.

'Anteater!' She spoke like Mickey.

'B-b-b- for what, Lucille?'

'Belly!' Zohra imitated Lucille's tone.

'Now listen, you all. C for calabash like them in Long Range Yard. D for donkey like Kalamadin donkey. E for eddo that Madeen always rootin' out. You hear me?'

This new alphabet delighted Zohra so much that she began to yell it at recess. Before long the children rejected their current favourite chant:

Arithmetic, arithmetic, me father sick,
Me mother gone to Crabwood Creek!

Instead, they took up Zohra's new alphabet. Miss Gusta soon felt the repercussions of Zohra's imagination.

'G for . . .?' she asked.

'Guana, miss,' cried Bebi. She meant *iguana*.

'Yes, dear. But what else it mean?'

Bebi looked crestfallen.

'G-r-a-,' Miss Gusta spelled out hopefully. But Zohra had unwittingly brainwashed the others and Bebi could not supply the answer their teacher wanted.

'Grass! Grass! What happen to you all? Start again. A for . . . ?'

'Anteater.'

'No, no! Apple that you eat at Christmas. And B for –?'

'Belly!'

Miss Gusta's head jerked up at the mention of the part of the anatomy that she delicately called 'tummy'. 'No, no! Bat. What about D?'

'Donkey.'

'Good. E?'

'Eddo.'

'E is for egg. Egg, you hear? Don't you remember?'

The children looked blankly at her.

'Don't tell me I wastin' me time with you!' she exclaimed in exasperation.

'But we forget, miss,' Claudie explained.

'Why?'

'Well, Zohra been tellin' us new ABC.'

Miss Gusta's face hardened into the texture of dead mango leaves. 'Why you makin' so much mischief, Zohra?'

'Me just say it at playtime and everybody want to know.'

'Awright! Stay in after school this afternoon and tell me all bout it.'

Everyone stared at Zohra for Miss Gusta seldom kept anyone in after school.

What wrong? Zohra thought. Why she vex with me?

At recess, instead of joining the other children on the veranda, the girl slunk away among the lime and guava trees. The stiff cleanliness of scrubbed boards and starched clothes that used to make Zohra feel at home now grew suffocating. She felt refreshed and safe among the trees. Zohra scrambled up onto the lowest branch of a guava tree. 'Is so nice here,' she breathed. 'It smell just like Miss Gusta!' Then she frowned. 'Why she so vex with me when me like she so much?'

She watched the sunlight trickle through leaves like gold dust, enhancing spiders' webs, mellowing limes and colouring her skin tea-brown. Zohra's upper lip and palms began to perspire. Her unhappiness oozed away. Still, a thoughtfulness remained, clinging to her mind as the moss did to the trees.

School bell ringing, Zohra thought. Miss Gusta will vex even more if me don't go.

At three that afternoon, the other children left Zohra sitting on the back bench, outweighed and dwarfed by her school bag. She still clutched her pencil-box, snapping it open and shut. Suddenly the box fell to the floor, disturbing Miss Gusta, who had been marking slates.

'Me didn't keep you here fo' make noises. Pick it up and keep quiet.'

Her stern voice demolished the little girl's courage. With tear-blurred eyes she stooped to collect her pencils. They lay on the floor, a scattered rainbow of colours. Slowly, Zohra gathered her pencils, confining them as she had done earlier with her imagination. She began to crack her knuckles.

Miss Joycie entered with a jug of swank. It was a hot afternoon. 'Eh, eh, is first time you keep in Zohra,' she observed, as she poured a glass for Miss Gusta.

'She been teaching them chil'ren the wrong alphabet,' Miss Gusta said.

'Oh, you bad lil' gal!' Miss Joycie cried. 'Wait till Miss Esther hear this. Essie! Sis! Come hear this!'

'Wait a minute,' Miss Essie said from the kitchen.

Zohra shivered. Miss Gusta quietly sipped her swank while Miss Joycie cleaned the blackboard. Zohra watched the particles of chalk fall from the board. They fell as dizzily as she had done from Miss Gusta's favour.

'What you all want?' said Miss Essie, as she came from the kitchen. Her head, borne up by her long body, seemed to move among the rafters. Slowly, she lowered her eyes to her sisters' level. 'What happen?'

'Mrs Fisul granddaughter been teaching them chil'ren wrong alphabet!'

'Me never hear the like in me born days, Sis Essie!' Miss Gusta blurted out. 'She sit so quiet too, then bam! She do this. Messin' up all me hard work. How Anglican school will have them chil'ren if they don't know alphabet?'

Miss Esther lowered her eyes considerably more to Zohra's level. 'Come here, chile,' she said.

Zohra raised her scared eyes to Miss Esther's face. Miss Esther seemed taller than ever. A few minutes earlier she had felt like chalk dust falling dizzily downwards. Now upwards. This seesaw of emotion stupefied her. She went to the three sisters.

'Repeat the alphabet for them,' Miss Gusta ordered.

Zohra's mouth opened but her voice refused to sound.

'Come on! You holler it enough at playtime. Show we how clever you are then,' Miss Gusta said.

'Go on,' coaxed Miss Joycie.

Miss Esther alone remained aloof.

Zohra tried again. She began at A and continued till her voice choked at I. 'J for jamoon,' she croaked. 'K for kiskadee.'

The words became muffled. Tears tumbled down her cheeks. 'Home – Gramma! Me want to go home!' Zohra cried.

'Why you cryin'?' Miss Gusta asked softly. 'We ain't beat

you. You got to learn you mustn't spoil other people work and make mischief. You all know, sisters, how me live fo' the Lawd, you all and the teachin'. Now she spoil everythin'.'

Upset as she was, Zohra yet sensed the hurt in Miss Gusta's voice. Then Miss Esther intervened. 'Quiet, Gusta,' she commanded. 'Sit down, Zohra. Wipe you eyes with this kerchief.'

She turned to her sisters. 'Me surprise at you colleaguing with Gusta, Joycie. She is a big woman now, but still spiteful like lil' chile. She get vex because Zohra teach them chil'ren something they like more than she own. Gusta, you think teachin' is playin' dolly house? You think chil'ren is plaything?'

'Mind what you say in front the chile, Essie!'

'Is best she learn while she lil', Joycie. Zohra, you keep all you hear to yourself. You hear me?'

Zohra nodded, mopping her eyes with Miss Esther's handkerchief.

'You hurt Miss Gusta feelings, tellin' them chil'ren new alphabet. You mustn't do it again, okay?'

'*No*. Me didn't know. Oh, me like Miss Gusta, oh!' She began to cry again. 'She always look so nice in she hat and stockin' and lace!'

'You ain't sorry, Gusta? Isn't you who always talking bout "suffer the lil' chil'ren"?' Miss Esther demanded.

Miss Gusta looked upset. 'Oh, Sis Essie!'

'And – she always smell so nice, like guava!' Zohra blubbered.

A low laugh halted the child's tears. She looked up. Miss Esther was laughing quietly, her tall frame shaking like the lime trees and her all-seeing eyes were shut. Zohra stopped crying, for she had never seen Miss Esther laugh. The child felt as though she were in the presence of a great phenomenon such as an earthquake or a flood.

'Guavas!' panted Miss Esther. 'Man, that beat everything! Gusta!'

Her body folded up like a deck chair as she sat down next to Zohra. Her two younger sisters began to laugh.

'Well,' said Miss Gusta at last. 'We better get you some of Miss Joycie nice sponge cake. Wait here.' Miss Gusta's eyes once more projected love. Zohra nodded happily.

'Zohra,' said Miss Esther gently, when her sisters had left the room. 'Me believe chil'ren must learn young. They is lil' grown-ups. You see, because Miss Gusta like teaching, she don't like anybody to interfere. So she vex when you teach them chil'ren the alphabet, but she too proud to see this. Me don't know if you can understand.'

Zohra's eyes grew larger; she still clutched the handkerchief and tried hard to understand. Miss Esther looked at her kindly. 'You make a good alphabet, but wait till you turn big to teach it.' Then she added, almost to herself, 'God send the chile to protect we from pride. Is true He say except you be lil' chil'ren, you can't enter the kingdom of heaven. He teach we this all over again.'

Miss Essie talkin' bout God again. But she so nice and make Miss Gusta like me again, Zohra thought.

Miss Esther's eyes encountered the child's at that moment. She smiled, but unlike Miss Gusta's smile, hers contained no vulnerability. It felt like the protection and the strength of the trees in the school garden that morning.

Anish Desai

ANISH DESAI was born in Birmingham. He has lived in various parts of the UK, studying and working. It was on his return to the city of his birth that he felt the need to pick up a pen and start writing. The stories in this anthology are his first to be published. He combines writing with teaching mathematics.

A Brimful of Hope

Anish Desai

With one hand, he fumbled for the keys in his pocket; with the other, he brushed aside the privet branches overhanging the path. At the front door, his hand shook, making the key scratch against the lock. At first, Manu thought it was a television with the volume turned up high, but soon he understood that the sound, the continuous howl, came from his own home. He tried to unlock the door, jabbing metal on metal. Eventually the lock turned. Inside the noise was louder – it ricocheted off the walls, intensifying, filling his home. He called out his wife's name. 'Asha! Asha!' Where is she? he thought. Manu dropped his briefcase and climbed the stairs, two at a time.

It was quiet as he entered the nursery. The baby whimpered, sniffing snot back up her nose as she inhaled. Would she start again if he picked her up? She seems happy now, he thought. He approached the cot cautiously, as if closing in on a bomb that might explode if he made a false move. 'It's okay, Uma. Daddy's here,' he said, taking another tentative step. The infant's eyes, red and water-filled, stared at him. Keep her attention and she'll stay calm, Manu thought. 'It's all right,' he repeated. As soon as he held out his arms to her, Uma began to scream. He swooped her up to his shoulder and jogged her in his arms, whispering, 'Hush, Uma. Hush.' He carried her to the window where they looked down at the garden. 'Look at the kitty,' he said, directing her attention to the fat tabby balancing on the fence. Cats usually brought pleasure to Uma, smiles and excited gurgles, but today the tabby was as good as invisible.

Manu searched for a toy to draw her attention. From the crib, he picked out a red, round figure with a circular antenna on its head and pushed it into his daughter's hand. The toy spoke 'Eh-oh!' as Uma clutched it loosely. As they returned downstairs, under the screaming in his right ear, Manu heard the toy say 'Big Hug!'

The living room was as he had left it that morning. An empty cup on a coaster. A plate with crumbs of toast on the coffee table. Nothing had been tidied up. *Where is she?* He glanced at the television, almost expecting it to be on, emitting white noise, that Hollywood omen of domestic disaster.

At the kitchen door, Manu stood, afraid to go further. Uma became tense in his arms. Her mouth was fixed open, the gathering noise unable to escape. Her mother sat on the floor, her arms resting on her knees, fragments of glass at her feet. The top of the bottle, the rubber teat encased in a plastic ring, had rolled towards the door, to where Manu's feet now were. Her trousers had become damp in the pool of milk. Asha's face was like her daughter's had been earlier.

'It won't stop,' she cried, one hand pushed hard into her forehead as if trying to force out the noise. 'Please make it stop.'

Since his teenage years, Manu had believed that his mother would choose his wife for him. She knew, after all, the qualities a future partner should have: a nature not too spirited nor too slow, not cheap in her dress or talk, and a natural ability to cook and clean. He had expected to be introduced to a number of girls, go on a series of nervous dates and then marry the one his mother recommended. Instead, as he entered his parents' living room, he was unsure who would be more surprised, him or his mother. Standing beside him, her hand in his, was Asha, her eyes directed to the floor as his mother studied her.

'Take a seat. Sit down please,' his mother said, pointing towards the sofa. Once seated, she placed her hand on Asha's cheek as if checking she was real, made of flesh and bones. Asha smiled. Her hands fidgeted in her lap. The older woman then took a young hand in hers and massaged it. She began asking questions to which Asha replied with simple words or small movements of her head.

His mother wore the deep blue cotton-print sari that he had seen at past weddings. On those occasions, Manu had considered her appearance majestic, but today, in the shimmer of rich ruby in Asha's silk sari and in the sparkle of gold necklace around his fiancée's neck, his mother looked ordinary.

His father sat in his usual armchair, his attention jumping from the television to the new girl in his house like a spectator at a tennis match. He wore grey trousers and a white shirt. The jacket was missing but Manu recognized the uniform his father had worn driving buses since arriving in England thirty years ago. He could have changed, Manu thought.

His parents' clothes wouldn't have seemed important a year ago when he was Asha's tutor, helping her with her statistics coursework. They had talked and laughed, drunk tea and scoffed Jaffa Cakes, each careful not to overstep the line of detached intimacy between teacher and student. After Asha had completed her degree, Manu surrendered to his desire to see her again and called her. While he counted the telephone rings, he focused on the cartoon face Asha had drawn next to her number.

'He hasn't changed a bit,' said Asha, cooing at a photograph of a baby Manu. Plates and uneaten snacks had piled up at the end of the coffee table. More albums were scattered across the rest of the table. It seemed like hours since the two women had begun Manu's life story with his parents' wedding in India. The faded black-and-white images showed guests staring at the camera with large eyes as if it threatened to take away their humanity. While they looked at the pictures, his mother told stories of her son as a sullen and lonely child, stirring within him forgotten memories and emotions.

Relief surged through Manu when his mother eventually shut the last album and placed it with the others. They sat quietly, not knowing what to say. Gunshots and horses galloping across sandy landscapes interrupted the silence. His father's eyes were closed and he snored gently. His mother rose to turn off the television, muttering that nobody was watching. Asha excused herself and asked Manu where the bathroom was. He led her to the foot of the stairs. As he watched his fiancée, he heard his mother whisper in his ear, 'She's lovely.'

His feet pounded into the sand in time with the rhythm of the waves washing the shore. Why had she married him? The doubts persisted. Since the wedding and now, days later, on a Spanish beach, they troubled him. What could she have found attractive in him? He had no talent that he was aware of, and was neither witty nor smart. He lacked ambition, satisfied with the cycle of work, food and sleep. Manu was aware that his languor was collecting around his waist and that his hair had begun to thin, a year before his thirtieth birthday. Asha had her youth, still only twenty-two. His was at an end.

A page rustled next to him. He recalled her parents' house, large and spacious, surrounded by well-kept lawn and towering trees, her bedroom full of keepsakes, soft toys and photos, and her wardrobes packed with past and present fashions. He could ask her these questions but the answers frightened him. A book fell to his side. He heard her ask if he was okay. Manu nodded. The lapping of the sea drew him to sleep, his feet buried in the hot sand.

That evening, Manu stood in front of the mirror in their hotel room. He held one shirt before him and studied the reflection. He tried another and noticed the indifferent response on the face in the mirror. Should he wear the blue cotton or the stripes tonight? The former matched his sombre mood. The other, Asha had picked out for him; to his surprise it suited him. The shirts fell to the bed. He returned to studying his reflection. When he breathed in, his stomach flattened. Breathing out, his paunch reappeared, making him look as if he'd swallowed a football. He inhaled and held his breath.

Cold hands grabbed the flesh above his belt. 'You don't have to do that. I like your tummy,' said Asha. Manu turned to face her. He put his arms around her, plump and soft, comfortable in her flesh, sweet and fragrant as if made from ripe mangoes. She rested her head on his shoulder, her hands moving gently over his back, in strokes warm and close.

A year after the wedding, Manu's father died, his arteries clogging up like his bus routes. After the funeral, Manu decided to spend three nights a week with his mother. On one of those evenings, as she prepared dinner, Manu noticed her remoteness. 'Are you thinking of Dad?' he asked.

'A little.' She placed a pot of potato curry on the kitchen table. They ate. 'I'm going to India.'

'To India. When?'

'In a month's time. I'll be going for the winter, not for a holiday.'

'For the whole winter,' Manu repeated. His mother looked more distant, as if she too was leaving him, fading away gently, not with the force with which his father had been torn away.

'I may do it every year. Spend the winter in India. All my friends are doing it.' She mentioned some names. 'Their children have grown up and got families of their own. They don't feel they belong to their new families.' She paused. 'I need good weather. Sunshine. Not these grey clouds every day. I want family around me. I want to see friendly faces when I go to the shops, not unhappy ones. I want to be able to stop in the street and chat to people. It's going to be so lonely in this house.'

Manu pushed his plate away and covered his face with his hands.

'I promise I'll come back in the summer to see you and Asha,' his mother said. She rose, walked around the table and stood behind him. 'I need this.' She placed a hand on his shoulder. 'You should start a family.'

That night, the blankets pressed down on him so he could feel the springs beneath him. His feet reached the end of the bed and no matter how much he struggled, he could not free the blanket tucked tightly under the mattress. He felt trapped, pinned down by the bedclothes.

As a child, his mother had taught him the *Gayatri* mantra. He had learned it by heart and would proudly recite it back to her. She told him that saying the words each night before sleep would create a protective shroud around him, keeping away the harm darkness could bring.

He had followed her advice. Now as he lay awake, remembering bullies at school, worries about money and exams while he was at university, he murmured the words.

Manu didn't cry at the airport. His mother assured him she'd return in May and bring him back a box of mangoes. She hugged him, trembling in his arms. They said their goodbyes. He didn't watch her walk through passport control. He didn't notice the damp patch on his shirt.

Manu returned to his mother's house. He marched along the carpet of sodden leaves on the path, past the For Sale board planted on the lawn. He turned the key and the door opened. Coats hanging in the hallway, shoes on the rack underneath, the framed picture of Sai Baba on the wall opposite – all had gone. The inviting aromas from the kitchen were replaced by still air. In the living room, the sofa was covered by a blanket. His father's armchair, so much moulded to his shape that it was impossible to sit on, had gone. Manu stared at the television as it refused to come alive. Then he remembered. Everything was cut off: electricity, gas, phone. He called the college on his mobile to ask if he could extend his leave. He stood in the middle of the room, surprised by the hollow sound of his voice.

As night drew in, Manu went to his bedroom, more out of habit than need. The walls were stripped of wallpaper and the floor of carpet. In the open window, the shadows of swaying branches were the dancing ghosts of his childhood. Manu lit a candle that he'd found in the emergency kit his mother kept in the kitchen. He ate a bag of stale crisps and lay down on his bed. The blankets had gone, donated to a charity in India. He felt there should have been a bottle for company, some cans at least, but he wasn't used to drinking alone. The candle flame flickered and died. He let his eyes get accustomed to the dark.

Manu discovered there was little he could do to occupy himself without electricity. No TV, no radio or music. He had never been much of a reader and now didn't feel like a good time to start. He feared venturing outside, going for a walk, browsing in shops, in case somebody recognized him, approached him and began a conversation. How *are* you? I haven't seen you for a while. I'm sorry to hear about your father. He didn't need their pity. He was content, alone in the house.

He watched the street through the window, pleased with how few pedestrians passed. There were old Indian women weighed down with shopping and fresh-faced students, talking excitedly as they walked. A silver BMW pulled up outside. The dark-suited driver opened his briefcase and checked some documents. It's the estate agent come to show the house to prospective buyers, Manu thought. Should he hide? Or could he explain that he had come round to check on the house? Before he could decide, the car sped off.

He needed to find a place to hide. On the landing, Manu noticed the hatch in the ceiling. Moments later, he pulled up the aluminium ladder and replaced the square piece of wood over the opening. The smell of old clothes lingered. He lay on the plywood floor, feeling the cold more than he could ever remember. He listened to his breathing. It seemed to be amplified as if there were others breathing with him. Manu sat up and looked around him into the perfectly black space. Nothing. A quarter of an hour later, shivering, the cold and dark creeping into him, he climbed down.

That evening Asha called at the house. 'I've got news,' she said, smiling. After the wordless days, Manu found his mouth could not form any. 'I've brought some food. Maybe we can eat first?' She raised a shopping bag full of plastic containers as proof. She smiled again, nervously this time.

Her hair was tied in a knot away from her face. She wore pale trousers and a pink top that Manu thought made her look fat. He wanted her to leave.

As she placed the contents of the bag on the kitchen surface, she spoke what seemed to Manu a string of unconnected words. 'You didn't answer my calls or texts. When are you coming home?' He felt her gaze upon him as if she was ordering him to look at her. 'Mum called,' she said. Manu looked up. 'She asked for you but I didn't know what to say. Why don't you come back after we've eaten and we can call her? It won't be too late. If we hurry, we should be able to catch her before she goes to sleep.' This was the good news. Now she could go.

Asha spooned food onto a plate, excited at the prospect of eating together. 'Here we are. Sit. Let's eat.'

Manu sat. He stared at the plate that Asha had placed before him. 'Is there something wrong?' she asked. 'It should still be hot.' Her voice shook. 'What's the matter? Why don't you say something? Say something.' She sat down next to him. She tore off a piece of chapatti, scooped curry into it and raised it to his mouth. 'Eat,' she pleaded. 'Please eat.'

'Do you have any salt?' Manu muttered.

'Salt? You haven't tasted it yet.' Asha ate the food in her hand. 'It's fine. It doesn't need salt.' Asha brought the plate closer to Manu. 'Eat!' Her face became distorted. 'It's good.' Tears emerged. The plate shook violently. Food fell into Manu's lap. The plate hit the floor, breaking as it did so. Asha began to cry. Manu sat silent, the oil in the food soaking his trousers. A fragment of crockery hit the cooker.

Asha dropped to her knees. Manu heard sobs as she moved about the floor, then a scream. He looked up to see blood trickle down her hand and onto the floor, forming perfect circles.

*

The mattress was bare and uneven. Ghosts danced in the window. Thoughts and images raced through his head, each linking, each ousting the last in a smooth revolution.

Om. Bhoor bhuvahswah. What's next? The end? The last line I know. *Dheemahi dhiyonaha prachodayat*. What comes in between?

She didn't say a word. She just tidied up and left.

The *Gayatri*. The missing lines. What are they? Try again. *Om. Bhoor bhuvahswah*. Dark circular spots on the floor. *Tat savitur varenyam*. Blood and tears. Tears and blood. *Bargho devasya*. She's gone. *Dheemahi dhiyonaha prachodayat*.

She's gone.

Again. *Om. Bhoor bhuvahswah* . . .

Uma sat on her grandfather's knee, picking at the grains of rice in his hand. Manu watched her across the dining table. Uma pointed to the plate that Bapa had finished eating from. The old man scooped a portion of rice and presented it to her. After Uma had finished, Bapa made a gesture with his hand to say no more. The infant copied him, holding up her hand and rotating her wrist with a concerned expression on her face. They burst into laughter together. She seemed so content, laughing and smiling. There were rare moments like this between Manu and his daughter. It was as if she too knew what he had done and excluded him from her joy.

Padma, Manu's mother-in-law, was clearing up after their meal. She returned from the kitchen and asked if Manu had finished – his meal, rice littered with cloves and cardamom pods and dhal awash with tamarind and bay leaves, was barely touched. Padma took the plates and returned to the kitchen. As she ran a tap over the plates, she called out, 'Is Asha still taking her tablets?' Manu replied that she was. 'She doesn't seem to be any better. I don't think they're working,' came a shout. 'We should see the doctor again.'

'The doctor said it takes two or three weeks for the drugs to take effect. Perhaps we should wait another week.'

Padma returned to the table, wiping her hands on a towel. 'I've never known her to sleep so much. That's not like her. She shouldn't be spending all day in bed. It can't be good for her.'

'Let her rest as much as she needs to. Uma and me are coping fine,' said Manu.

Padma sneered behind his back. 'She should be at home. Where I can look after her properly.'

'She is at home,' muttered Manu. She chose to come back, he thought.

'I don't think Asha feels that way. She knows she would be better off . . .'

Bapa called out his wife's name and she was quiet. Bapa's expression was stern, as if he were a judge about to pass sentence on a condemned prisoner. 'I think we should be going soon,' he said. He then spoke to his wife in Gujarati. Padma answered back, creating more noise as she worked. Manu, unable to follow their conversation, watched his daughter tug at her grandfather's tie. Bapa spoke short, hard words and the argument was finished. The old man turned to Uma with a benign expression. 'But first we have to say goodnight to my favourite girl,' he said in baby-English. Uma gurgled while she tried to grasp his spectacles.

An hour later, Bapa and Padma checked on their sleeping daughter. Manu thanked his mother-in-law for caring for Uma and Asha during the day. Padma acknowledged him with a gesture of the head, avoiding eye contact. He knew she would return the following day, the days after that, spending more and more time in his home, with his wife and daughter.

It was past Uma's usual bedtime when his in-laws left. Manu turned on the hot water tap to add to the two inches of cold water in the bath. The absence of routine wasn't good for her, he knew, but this was the only part of the day he could spend alone with Uma. He was not going to let Padma bathe her, despite her repeated requests. She was *his* child, his responsibility. Uma's hands swam through the water. 'Is the water hot?' Manu asked. 'Hot?' Uma shook her head. He scooped water into a plastic beaker and poured it over Uma. Shocked, she rubbed her eyes and continued her search for toys, twisting her body one way, then another. Manu found the soap but whenever he brought the bar near, Uma whimpered and shook her head. After several attempts, Manu gave up. He sat on the toilet seat and watched Uma splashing and playing with the coloured toy dolphins.

As he dressed Uma for bed, she waved her arms and kicked her legs. Manu wrestled with her, appealing for her to be still. Once she was in her Winnie-the-Pooh pyjamas, she grinned as if they'd been playing a game. Manu held her in his arms, rocking her gently, her head resting on his shoulders. After ten minutes of pacing across the nursery, Uma was still bright and alert. 'What are you smiling at?' Manu asked. The smile died and Uma stared into the corner of the room, where two walls met the ceiling. It was as if she could see things he couldn't: spirits, guardians of the realm where the unborn live, beckoning her to return. 'What is it? Is somebody there?' Manu kissed her cheek. 'Stay with me, Uma. I love you.' Manu placed her in the crib. He put near her the cloth dolls his mother had brought on her last visit, of Krishna and the patient Radha, both dressed in fine clothes as if they were to be wed. 'Goodnight. Sleep well.' He kissed her again.

*

The room was dark, the only light coming from a bedside lamp. Manu sat on the edge of the bed and placed his hand on Asha's heaving body, an amorphous mass rising and falling like a stormy sea. His wife had told the doctor that she felt like a log adrift in the ocean with Uma safe on an island, but she couldn't reach her or didn't want to. Her breathing was heavy, as if each breath needed effort. Manu pictured her as driftwood being smashed against the rocks by huge waves. He felt as helpless as when he'd found her in the pool of milk.

Normally, once Uma had settled, Manu would return downstairs to watch television into the early hours. Afraid to go to bed, he'd sleep on the couch. Tonight he felt the need to stay with his wife, to be close to her, at least physically. He was unsure what he could do, fearing that whatever he did would be wrong and only bring more harm. She'd come to his mother's house to share what the doctor had confirmed. Pregnancy. That had been the good news. The scar was visible, an inch long across her palm, where she'd caught the edge of the broken plate.

The lamp cast light upon a book. Manu picked it up. He ran a finger across the cover layered with dust, revealing the embossed gold lettering of the title, *A Brimful of Hope*. A pair of legs dressed in black stockings stretched across the letters, the body and head cut off by the edge of the book. Under the title, a quote promised 'a rollicking good read'. Manu opened it where the folded corner of a page marked where Asha had stopped reading. He began to read: *Jake was heartbreakingly pretty. His sun-bleached hair flopped into his eyes and his skin was a darker gold than the fields in which he worked.* Manu suppressed a laugh. He decided to read aloud, hoping this would discourage him from sneering. Next to him, Asha sighed. Manu filled the room with his careful reading. As he turned the pages, the words no longer bothered him. He was immune to their banality, even beginning to share the characters' indulgences, their preposterous dreams, as if seeing his own frustrated desires in action. Asha's interest in these books became clear to him.

After twenty pages, Manu stopped. He sensed he was being watched intensely, like the thirty pairs of eyes staring at his back while he wrote on the whiteboard at college. Asha's eyes, which for so long hadn't seen with such intimacy, were open, focused on Manu and the book. The bedroom was still. Asha's breathing was more refined and the outline of her body had softened.

'Can you read some more?' she whispered.

Manu looked at the object in his hands as if he'd been caught with pornography. 'You want me to read?' he said. Asha nodded. 'Give me a minute. I need to get a drink.' He left the room and returned with two glasses of water. He placed one next to Asha. She took a sip. Manu climbed into bed beside her and drank his in one gulp. He placed the empty glass on the table beside him.

'I had to stop in the middle of a chapter. Do you want me to carry on?' he asked. 'Or go back to the beginning?'

'Why don't you start at the next chapter?'

Busy Minds Are Blind

Anish Desai

He had sat in the dark for over an hour. He'd got used to the fact that he couldn't see anything except for the gold border around the door and the grey shadows around him. He'd got used to the damp, earthy smell that reminded him of his towel after his bath. He'd got used to the silence, the stillness, with only his breathing, in and out, reminding him that he was still there in the cupboard under the stairs.

If he stayed here long enough, the boy wondered, would he disappear? He could turn into a small animal, a mouse maybe, scurrying along walls, feeding off breadcrumbs and pieces of cheese. He imagined how his life would be if he lived here as a mouse. Would his mother notice if he disappeared? She would have to tell the police, who would come round with sniffer dogs and search the whole house. And his mother would cry when the police told her that they couldn't find him.

He began to lose the sensation in his legs. He stretched them and wriggled his toes. They were alive after all. His hand moved along his bare leg, up to his bony knee. He ran a finger over it, feeling the deadness of a scab compared to his soft skin. He picked at the edges of the dried crust. It will never heal if you pick at it, he could hear his mother say, and he stopped. Silence. It had been some time since he'd heard the doorbell and then his mother's nasal, slightly whining voice. More women's voices mixed so that it was impossible to tell them apart. Soon the chatter faded. Shortly after, he heard a clinking sound. Plates with slices of cakes, he guessed. Then everything was quiet again.

His hand moved over the wall, the brickwork, the rough surface with a grid of grooves. A finger slipped into a channel that was smoother than the brick but still coarse to his skin. His finger ran along the channel like a car. At a T-junction it turned and followed the road upwards, making its way through a network of imaginary roads. The scrabbling of furious paws at the door, the scratching of desperate claws against the wooden frame brought the journey to an end. There was a proud meow. He sat as quiet as he could. Then he heard the pitter-patter of feet making their way towards the kitchen. This was what he enjoyed most about being in the cupboard. No one and nothing could disturb him or invade his private den. At first, he used to hide in the cupboard after his mother had scolded him. The stillness acted against her cruelty, her refusal to listen to what he had to say. *I didn't break the vase – it fell. The scratch on the table was already there – my truck didn't do it.* He enjoyed the quiet in the cupboard. It seemed to filter into him, flowing through him, pushing out the monster that made his hands shake, made him scream and bawl, made him want to break his toys. After being in the cupboard, he felt the quiet inside him, as if his belly was full of ice cream, the coolness spreading through him into his arms and legs. And nothing his mother said could take the feeling away.

His hand reached out to touch a cool, metal cylinder. The lid fell as he dragged the can towards him. A chemical smell escaped. He recognized it from the time men in white uniforms that covered their arms and legs had come to the house. They had worn matching white hats. They had hidden the downstairs rooms under large blankets. Everything became obscured: chairs, tables, desks, television. His mother had told him to stay in his bedroom while the men were here. *You don't want to be a distraction to them. They are going to be very busy, they have work to do*, she'd said. *You'll only cause a mess*. While his mother spoke, the men were laughing at him. Unable to bear their teasing smiles, he decided to stay in his bedroom, where they were not invited.

On each day that the painters worked at the house, the sun shone brilliantly, the windows concentrating the rays so the sun seemed to burn him directly. No matter where he sat in his room, he found it difficult to escape the sun, which would eventually catch up with him. In the end, he spent his time crouching in the space between the bed and the wardrobe, invisible hands leaving him food that he would shovel into his mouth.

By the time the men left, rows of soldiers lay in front of him, rows of moulded green and grey figures, missing limbs and heads, with torsos split in half, their military tanks and jeeps crushed and mangled. Streams from pools of red, blue and black ink joined to form a scarlet river that wound its way around the scattered pieces of plastic. His hands, stained red, held the fragments of his broken pens.

When his mother came into his bedroom to tell him that the men had left, he recognized her look.

'Tasso! Are you hiding in the cupboard again? Get out of there!'

The door opened but there was no one outside. It had

been a voice without a body. Tasso closed his eyes to protect himself from the light, allowing them time to adjust to the comparative brilliance. He crawled on his hands and knees to the door, wobbling and staggering into the hall. Hot air floated into the hall from the kitchen. It settled upon him, pressing on him, pushing and pulling him, urging him to do things he didn't want to do. His hands trembled. He wanted to scream his name to fill the hot silence. But then he remembered the cool feeling in his belly.

Voices from the drawing room attracted him. 'Gran will be here in ten minutes,' he cried, running around the table where ladies sat playing cards.

'Yes, dear,' said his mother keeping her eyes on her hand. 'Can't you see we're busy?'

'But I'm going to the zoo.'

'Yes, I know,' said his mother, rearranging her cards. 'Could you wait in your room?'

Tasso watched the ladies, their hands holding fans that veiled their faces. All he could see were eyes, cold like glass marbles, staring at playing cards. He understood there was little chance of disturbing their game. Tasso recognized two of the women, Mrs Gosh and Mrs Nice-Lovely, but he did not know the fourth lady's name. They were regular visitors. He couldn't remember when he had last seen his mother alone; she always seemed to be accompanied by one of them.

The women resumed their conversation. 'You must be happy with the amount we collected last week, Beatrice,' said Mrs Gosh.

'Yes, it was a reasonable amount. Over three thousand pounds for Cancer UK,' replied Tasso's mother.

'We should nominate you for an award for the work you do,' suggested Mrs Gosh. 'I think it's time you were recognized. I shall have to talk to the Mayor's wife.'

Mrs Nice-Lovely agreed excitedly. The fourth lady played her hand.

'There's no need. My friends appreciate me enough. I'm more concerned about setting up our next engagement. I was thinking about inviting the WI.'

'A super idea,' began Mrs Nice-Lovely.

'You deserve some recognition, Beatrice,' interrupted Mrs Gosh. 'You're an important member of the community. I feel it's time everybody knew of your activities. How you fill the social calendar and raise money for charity at the same time astounds me.'

The fourth lady, her long face curved like the man in the moon, looked at her hand through spectacles balanced halfway up her nose, occasionally peering over them to check on the other players. For a moment, Tasso felt that she was looking directly at him. *Leave. You are ruining the game*, she seemed to say. Tasso left for his room.

The last two numbers on his racing car clock were both fives. Not long until Gran arrives, he thought. He stared at the red digits and willed them to change. Unsuccessful, he picked up a comic and, sitting on his bed, flicked through the pages. He'd already read it, digested the stories and solved the puzzles. Tasso threw it to the floor and walked over to his toy cupboard. He scanned the contents but nothing aroused his imagination, each item appearing as dull as the next. Tasso checked the time. Had it changed since he last looked? Maybe it had stopped, he thought. Maybe Gran had arrived and was waiting for him. Tasso returned downstairs.

'Is Gran here?' he asked his mother. 'She should be here by now. She's always on time.'

'Not yet. A few minutes,' replied his mother. The fourth lady turned around and looked over her glasses. Tasso didn't ask any more questions.

The front door opened and closed. 'Gran's here!' said Tasso excitedly.

'That was your father.'

'Father was here?'

'He stopped by to collect some documents. He has a round of golf with a client this afternoon.'

'He could have taken me to the zoo.'

'You know your father is under a lot of work at the moment. He wouldn't have considered it anyway. Personal excursions aren't tax deductible.'

Tasso went to the window and looked out. Where is she? He turned to look at the clock on the wall, its pendulum swinging to mark the time. The minute hand was pointing straight up.

At last he saw the familiar tall figure. 'Gran's coming,' he yelled.

'Shoot!' said his mother, throwing her cards to the table. 'Tasso, can't you be quiet?'

'Ten, nine, eight . . .' Tasso began.

'Quiet!' The other women muttered their disapproval as his mother gathered the cards to deal the next hand.

'. . . four, three, two, one.'

Ding-dong!

Tasso closed his eyes. The sounds of the bus zooming towards the zoo filled his head. He popped a sweet into his mouth and waited to discover his choice. Strawberry. His favourite. One summer evening came to mind, the cool sun falling behind the house, and his grandmother serving strawberries and ice cream, the sweet fruit fresh and chilled. That was the day Gran had bought the pigs. A black one and a white one. A male and a female. Pot-bellied, she called them. They had moved about their pen on stubby legs. Their bodies were spotted with dirt and sticks of straw but the pigs seemed unconcerned. Their faces were squashed as if they had walked into a wall, noses wrinkled and wet.

'What are their names?' Tasso asked, stretching his arm out, hoping to touch one of the pigs, whose faces came up to his waist.

'Troilus and Cressida,' replied his grandmother.

'Hello, Toyless.'

Tasso's hand patted the pig's hide. It was hard and tough, with hairs like the broom bristles in the cupboard under the stairs. Troilus grunted and walked away, leaving Tasso's hand hanging in the air. His grandmother scattered pellets from a paper sack into the pen. On it were the words Pig Chow and a picture of a pink pig eating from a trough. The pigs sniffed the ground, picking out food from straw and leaves with satisfied grunts. Once he had finished eating, Troilus walked to a corner of the pen, where he did his toilet. When his white partner had finished, she too went to the corner.

'Do they always go there?' Tasso said, pointing.

'Of course,' Gran said, in a tone that suggested it absurd to think otherwise.

'But I thought they liked to play in muck,' he said. He heard his mother's voice in his mind. *Are you playing in filth again? Are you a pig?*

'Pigs play in mud so they don't get too hot.'

His mother had lied. Pigs aren't dirty. Pigs aren't greedy. Maybe if she came to meet the pigs, she would change her mind.

The bus slowed as it approached the high street. I hope I see the pigs again after we've been to the zoo, Tasso thought. He was fond of them, more than Jasper the cat, a fluffy black-and-white ball, more than the sheepdog that reminded him of a man in a scruffy suit, more than any of the other animals his grandmother had bought since her vacation. Tasso often asked about her holiday, but she would rub her hands instead of answering. His mother had said that it was exactly what she had needed, the best care money could buy, and that it had done her a lot of good.

As a bus passed in the opposite direction, the driver raised his thumb. Tasso noticed the driver of his bus raise his hand. Another bus approached and the drivers gestured to each other with serious faces. This was important to them, as important as driving the buses themselves. More buses passed and each time the driver raised his hand while his fellow drivers saluted in return. It didn't matter if the buses were different colours or if they were travelling different routes, the drivers greeted each other as if they belonged to a special club. A bus approached and as it passed, the driver raised a hand and winked. Several seats behind the driver's cab, the six-year-old boy raised his thumb, the latest member of the bus drivers' club.

By the time Tasso reached the final exhibit at the zoo, he sensed the badness within him, the monster he had tried to hide in the cupboard under the stairs. It had ripped the paper bag in his pocket into crude flakes of confetti. The shopkeeper's smile, his joy at watching Tasso looking excitedly across the line of bottles filled with sweets and candies, were lost and forgotten. Fine white powder emptied into his pocket, the last sweet slipping into the sugary dust.

The lions had slept. The monkeys had squabbled. The parrots would not talk. And Tasso had to return home. He was not going to see the pigs. His mother had arranged a dinner and it was important that he attend. His grandmother had told him she didn't want to upset his mother, so he should go home. He knew his mother would stare.

Where are your table manners, Tasso! You eat like a pig.
He wanted to eat like a pig, choosy, with a sense of enjoyment and satisfaction. Tasso could not understand why he had to pretend to be somebody else, a boy who ate correctly, who was neat and smiled politely. Why did he have to be this monster?

The cupboard under the stairs seemed far away.

Quietly, Tasso and his grandmother made their way towards the exit. As they passed the Monkey House, where the monkeys screeched, they turned left and found themselves in an alley. Its untidy appearance and the smell of animal sweat and waste gave the impression that this was a forgotten part of the zoo. Only a young couple strolling ahead of them confirmed that it was open to the public.

Along one side was a line of cages, some occupied, some empty. Tasso noticed the sad orang-utans, their features wrinkled and withered, and the monkeys whose noses drooped down to their bellies, their eyes tired as if they'd had enough of being objects for laughter.

On the last cage in the line, a makeshift sign suggested that it was a temporary matter, an exhibit with no plans to stay for any length of time, something simply to fill the space. The ground was dry and dusty, a trickle of water from a nearby hose disappearing into the hungry soil. Litter and dead leaves hopped around with the wind, some landing inside the cage and continuing their dance there.

The words on the sign were in black paint, splashed onto a rotten wooden board. *The Invisible Man. Dare you see him!!!* Tasso felt his hand taken into his grandmother's, hard and cold on the edges, warm in the middle. She pulled his small hand away, towards home, towards safety, away from whatever she feared was in the cage. His other hand grasped the railing, tight. He wanted to stay.

The couple walked past. 'What's in this cage?' said the girl, pausing to look.

'Come on, we haven't time,' said her boyfriend. 'We have a train to catch. We said we'd be at Mum and Dad's for seven.'

'But I don't see anything in there.'

'That's because there's nothing there to see, silly,' said her boyfriend.

'Then why have an empty cage?'

'The sign's probably somebody's idea of a practical joke. Let's go.'

The girl stood her ground, as eager as Tasso to see the Invisible Man. The boyfriend sighed and looked at his watch.

Tasso looked into the cage. In a corner, he made out the dark outline of a manlike beast. It sat with its arms wrapped around its legs, its head nodding in the space between its knees, as if it had been there for ever. The cage was empty except for the dancing leaves.

Tasso squeezed his grandmother's hand. 'I can see something,' he whispered.

'I can too,' she replied.

'Then why can't anybody else?'

'Because busy minds are blind.'

The boyfriend made another attempt to encourage the girl to leave, but she shrugged him off. He began to walk away.

Tasso's free hand burrowed into his pockets, diving into the pit of sugar. He picked out the sweet smothered with icing sugar. He thought about eating it but instead he threw it into the cage, immediately feeling a sharp pull on his coat. The sweet landed in the middle of the cage on the bed of straw scattered across its floor. Tasso heard a shrill laugh from the girl.

The beast looked up to see what had landed in its cage. When it saw the sweet, it stood up. After days of crouching, standing proved difficult. The beast wobbled and staggered. It fell onto its hands and knees and crawled towards the sweet. Half the cage was bathed in sunlight and when the beast entered the brightness, it sprang back, its eyes unaccustomed to the light. It let them adjust and then entered the sunlight, where it sat, getting used to the warmth.

Moments later its hands began to shake, a few fingers at first, then arms and elbows and shoulders. Was it crying or laughing? The girl screamed. Her boyfriend ran to her and put his arm around her. 'What's the matter, love?'

'I think, I think I see *it*,' the girl said.

'Don't be silly. There's nothing there.' He held her tightly. 'There's nothing there. It's just your imagination.' He gave her a reassuring kiss and they walked away, the girl covering her face with her hands, the boy holding her, unable to console her.

Tasso's eyes widened. He wondered what had caused the beast's hands to shake. It's angry, he thought. It wants to break free from its cage, snap the bars in two. It wants to get at those who had awakened it, maybe those who had put it in the cage. Tasso shared the girl's fear, but he did not let it affect him. He stood, watching, his hand in his grandmother's.

When the beast noticed its shaking hands, it looked at them as if for the first time. The trembling stopped. Its gaze moved across the cage floor over the ordinary wooden boards to Tasso's bright red gift. The beast carefully picked a solitary piece of straw off the sweet. As it was about to place it in its mouth, it stopped. Tasso and the beast looked at each other. Tasso removed his hand from his pocket and dropped shreds of paper onto the ground. A breeze picked them up and carried them away, fluttering and gambolling. A familiar ice-cream coolness settled upon him.

The beast placed the sweet in its mouth. Its body relaxed as it sucked, as if a lost pleasure had returned. It lifted its hand and held it there. Tasso raised his thumb in return.

Bobby Nayyar

BOBBY NAYYAR was born in Handsworth in 1979. He studied French and Italian at Trinity College, Cambridge, and then Comparative Literature at the University of Chicago. He has worked in Europe and the Far East. He trained at Faber and Faber and currently works at Little, Brown.

The Syndicate of Tears

Bobby Nayyar

At about eight-fifteen each weekday morning, Babu Singh would pull up his white transit van near the end of Craythorne Avenue and beep the horn three times. BEEP BEEEEP BEEP. Everybody in the surrounding area knew what it meant. The disapproving faces hidden behind white curtain lace would look at the house and wonder why the recipient never waited outside.

Her reason was obvious: she hated going to work. Her children called the driver Bo-Peep because he always came to round up his sheep and take them to the factory. His employees, all of them women, chose a name that was not decent or easily translatable. Prabjhot Kaur would say that name three times before she opened the front door and loaded herself into the van. She was usually the last of seven women on the round-up, and so would end up squatting by the double doors and being crushed by the force of the other women when Babu turned a corner too sharply.

Babu owned and ran his own coat-making factory in a rundown part of Handsworth. He had bought the creamy-white building many years ago on the cheap, and had never renovated or modernized it. The ground floor was used to keep stock and materials, while the first floor was where the women worked on their sewing machines and other

63

contraptions. Babu also had an office, but spent most of his time keeping an eye on the ladies or delivering the coats to different locations. The floors of the building had splendid colourful tiles, and the high ceilings had their original wooden beams, but nobody noticed.

In the short assembly line, it was Prabjhot's job to sew on zips and buttons. For three months or so the factory would make the same coat, usually in anticipation of the changing seasons. This time around it was waxy green bomber jackets. Babu afforded his workers a radio so they could listen to Asian music, but the sound was usually drowned out by the pinpoint hammering of the different machines. At Prabjhot's eye-line all she could see was waxy green. She imagined that she was in a field or forest somewhere, free to walk and rest at her leisure. She knew that she had to focus because she didn't want to have to unstitch and redo any of her work. Sometimes the needle went through her finger. After many years it didn't hurt as much as it once did.

Babu was Prabjhot's brother-in-law and this familial connection kept her locked in the factory. Most of the women were also tied to it in a similar way. They were the wives of friends and relatives, some of them old and not able to remember life any differently, others young and recently arrived from India – women with crushed red lipstick and kohl who wondered why their lives had become so circumscribed by marriage and money. For the men involved it was an ideal situation; they could feel secure in the knowledge that Babu would pick up their wives, keep an eye on them and then deliver them back home around five.

For Prabjhot it was a case of being alone with people but free to populate her world with thoughts. She was thirty-

six years old with two children who went to secondary
school. Work gave her cash in hand, part of which she kept
for herself, depositing it in an old steel tin, tucked at the
back of a drawer. Her husband knew about the tin and
would open it up from time to time to count the money, but
he never dared take any because he knew that a greater
sum would then disappear from one of his stashes. The
money carried the same smell of oil, incense and raw
fabrics as the factory.

Over the years Babu had found different ways to moti-
vate his workers, such as buying them food and taking
them on a short trip once a year. His latest idea was to take
one pound from each woman's weekly salary and buy her
a lottery ticket. He would choose the numbers himself and
place the tickets in the greasy envelopes he used to hand
out the cash. On the surface it was a pleasant, if condes-
cending, gesture. The women accepted the tickets with
restrained gratitude, each one hoping with all her heart that
she would win and not have to come into work on Monday. Every now and then someone would win ten pounds
or close to a hundred, but that was it. Nobody believed
that they would win the jackpot.

Then it happened. No, not that. Fourteen million to one!
That's like all the stars in the sky, all the fish in the sea.
Prabjhot's ticket had five of the six numbers. She was rich
but all she did was carefully fold the ticket and place it in
her steel tin. Partly out of shock and disbelief, she simply
carried out the rest of her Saturday night duties, her husband drunk and unaware dozing on the settee, her children locked in their room playing computer games. It was
her secret, but some streets away Babu was furious. He
had taken his red turban off so he could tug at his hair. He
always knew the numbers he picked for his workers. One

of them had netted £750,000. He tugged and pulled, then remembered that it was Prabjhot's, his brother's wife. The money should be his.

Meanwhile, Prabjhot checked and checked the ticket over again, finally taking it from the tin, writing her name and address on it and then stashing it in a jar full of fennel seeds in the kitchen. The phone had rung several times. She unplugged it.

The night lay still as if it were a wall between her husband and her. Prabjhot got up and quietly pulled the curtains open. She looked out the window at the moon and the garden below, then took a cursory glance at the neighbour's new patio furniture. She raised an eyebrow and sighed, turned and sat on a chair. She watched her husband sleep in the silver-tinted glow, his bulbous stomach rising and falling like a whale surfacing for air. He was a thin man when she first met him, a few days before their wedding. Thin and neat with carefully ironed trousers and an engineered smile. The rivers of excitement and expectation that coursed through her in those days felt like love, but those rivers ran to no sea. Their conjugal bed was covered with flowers that were pressed to the sheets and brushed to the floor in haste, pregnancy coming before their wedding gifts had even been put away. Prabjhot sat and watched her husband's distended stomach and considered that he had been pregnant for many years, pregnant with sloth and envy and too many parathas. She thought of the lottery ticket, folded and hidden in the fennel seeds – she could take it and steal away into the night. Live a separate life. She held up the thought as if it were an object glinting in the moonlight and then crawled back into bed.

Sunday morning came and Prabjhot retrieved the ticket when she went to make tea. She stood over the stove and dropped some fennel seeds into the pot, along with a few cardamom seeds and black cloves. She glanced around the cramped kitchen. The fitted cupboards had never been replaced – they looked like the illegitimate children of a 1970s MFI display – and the walls were covered with a sticky residue of grease and turmeric. She envisioned the cupboards being torn down and replaced, and then the wall being torn down and the room extended. She blinked and imagined herself in a new house with space for a washing machine, a tumble-dryer and a dishwasher. She had put the ticket under the fold of her bra, which was a place where few men would dare to enter.

Mahendra Singh, Prabjhot's husband, drank his tea with such hypnotic, measured slurps that his wife found it difficult to reveal her good news. Finally, when he was finished, she touched the hem of her salwar kameez and told him that she had won some money. He shrugged his shoulders and then persisted in chewing a soggy cardamom seed. '*Kineh*?' he asked.

Prabjhot told him, and he started to choke. Under the beard, moustache and eyebrows, his face was a bright red, which matched the turban resting on a table. Mahendra asked to see the ticket. His wife reluctantly reached in and handed it to him, feeling glum and resigned as if she had already handed over the money. Her husband checked the numbers on teletext; the ticket seemed to disappear in his hand. Prabjhot's heart sank. The doorbell rang three times and the pair woke from their thoughts of happiness and despair. Much to their surprise, Mahendra handed back the ticket to his wife and told her to stash it in the same place. With renewed optimism he got up, put on his turban and strode to the front door. He expected that it would be his brother.

*

Babu had spent the night cursing and devising different schemes to get the money. He alternated between the living room and the bedroom, checking the teletext and other news services. The skin above his beard puffed and became dry, the space below his eyes developed purple rings. He was a man spurned and detested by fate. He had ignored his younger brother and had gone alone in creating and running his business. Now it was Mahendra who had enough wealth to quit his menial job and return to India as a king. It made perfect sense that of all his workers he would present this gift to the person who would cause the most damage. Babu hadn't even thought about Prabjhot. His protestations at the TV and his curses at his unanswered phone calls roused his wife, Radha. She tiptoed downstairs in her nightgown, walked into the living room and clasped his hands tightly. '*Chuup*,' she whispered into his ear, the breath stale but to him fragranced with ideas and inspiration. He knew what he would do when the morning came.

He stood at his brother's house and rang the doorbell three times. He had decided that he would just ask for fifty per cent of the winnings, as an investment, and then haggle from there. Mahendra opened the door slowly but fully so he could enjoy the pained expression on his brother's face. Babu held out a white box of laddu and other sweets, which he handed over as a sort of entrance fee. Mahendra moved aside and followed his brother to the living room. Prabjhot was in the hallway and caught the devious look on her brother-in-law's face. She bailed into the kitchen and started to make another pot of tea.

Mahendra had closed the living-room door with a deft smacking sound, which signalled his wife to stay in the kitchen. It didn't matter very much, as she could hear their words quite clearly. She listened as the pair skipped over pleasantries, then Babu launched into a prepared speech about how he wanted to expand the business and how he would like to involve his brother in this new enterprise. Babu coughed and spluttered as he mentioned the lottery win. His brother stayed silent as if not to taint each squirm and convulsion of his kin.

Then the real subject was broached as Babu asked that around £400,000 be invested. Mahendra waited a few seconds to see his brother quiver, and then started to laugh. He took a laddu from the box and broke it in two, handing the smaller half to his brother. Babu took the laddu gingerly and watched crumbs of flour and spices fall to the carpet. It tasted bitter as ashes, and he felt the complexion of his face turn red and yellow. The conversation was over.

Prabjhot waited for a prolonged silence before entering the living room. She was holding a flower-patterned steel tray with Soho Road fine china teacups, a spread of biscuits and a small bowl of sugar. Babu saw the false display of grandeur and stifled a humph. He stood up as Prabjhot rested the tray on the table. Babu gave some work-related excuse and left the house. He would have to use plan B.

Mahendra took another cup of tea and started to work his way through the Indian sweets. He looked up at his wife and asked to see the ticket once more. Prabjhot curled her fingers and touched her chest. She realized that she would have to conduct negotiations of her own.

Monday morning came and the white transit van crawled slowly to its usual nesting place on Craythorne Avenue. Babu was late, as he had spent the last ten minutes explaining to the other women how they could each get a share of the winnings. He had decided that they should work as a syndicate and thus take an equal share of the money. At first the women were genuinely reluctant as they were pleased that at least one of them had had some luck, but as

Babu continued to spout his bile, the women became more embittered. Six innocent, brown-faced, salwar kameez-chunni- and cardigan-wearing women turned into a tribe of baying savages, waiting in the back of an aluminium cage for Prabjhot to come. Babu beeped the horn three times and waited. There was no response and he, and the rest of his pack, started to panic. He pulled up the hand-brake and got out and rang the doorbell. There was no answer. He stepped across and peered through the front-room window. Everything was where it should be. He thought about ringing their number but knew there would be no answer. He turned around and looked at his van. He imagined that his pumped-up workers were now restless and expectant. He was their mouthpiece and their ass. He took a step forward to his badly parked van and then stopped and gasped for air. He wasn't ready to get kicked by a bunch of women.

Handsworth Songs

Bobby Nayyar

You are born into a country where your father works and does not believe in a god. This has a profound effect on you throughout your life. You think of religion as a painting on your shoes, clearly visible and certainly colourful, but something you can take off at any time. Other people see you in a different light. When you travel they see a Muslim, when you eat they see a Hindu, when you grow a beard they see a Sikh. You are born in a hospital either side of five thousand miles. You are walking away from Victoria Square, down New Street at a quarter past five on a sunny Tuesday afternoon. The sun is still high in the sky. It seems to smart your skin as you walk. The sea of people is grey and occasionally silver. You follow them down, as if drawn to tide by their thoughts.

You live in a city that died in your youth, was buried beneath concrete and newsprint. You left that city to trail in the wake of your aspirations, left it like a punctuation mark, a pause, only to come back and see it reborn. More than that, you see your city as the ouroboros of England – vast and unfolding, constantly devouring itself with new life. It has changed so much that you find yourself questioning everything you see, like the past has been rearranged in your absence. Yet your memories remain as echoes to your footsteps as you walk those familiar streets and whispers to your ear as you sleep in your childhood bed. New Street is busy. The tide stretches out and water washes far across the sand and then recedes and recedes. You wonder where it all goes at night. You are hungry and you want to go home.

Every year someone asks you why you don't believe in a god. This frustrates you and makes you think that your skin colour is a religion in itself. One time you use this to your advantage and feel ashamed for months afterwards. The gossamer thread of your mysticism is spun by your mother, told in tales of people of blue and pink skin. You once wore that string devoutly and then washed it away. You are walking at the pace of the people around you. They are black, white and brown, all of them workers like you, and they rush to their cars and buses. You feel suffocated by time. You shuffle your way diagonally through the crowd and take one of the side streets up from New Street. You are walking towards the cathedral.

You are seven and standing in a corner-shop queue. A white man is smoking in front of you. He is tired by the wait and tired of the people who have come to surround him from street to street. In the quietest form of protest, he turns and flicks ash onto your bare forearm. The hot greying dust startles you, as if waking you from a beautiful dream, but you do and say nothing. It is the first moment in which you realize that you can be defined by your difference. Singled out without saying a word. From then on you lose count of those moments. Ten years later you are offered your first cigarette. You refuse vehemently and then despise the offerer.

The pavement is narrow and you have to weave past people who are walking down to join the mass on New Street. You look at the faces of the women; they look at you in reaction to your attention but nothing more. In the shade of the narrow, tall buildings you feel some protection from the sun. The sky is a powder-dry blue.

When you are ten you come closer to understanding the notion of race. You visit a friend's house with another boy. The friend leaves you to get some drinks. You look at his room; it is a similar size to your own but has a strange smell: a mixture of incense and sewing-machine oil. The furniture is old and dusty. Your host has dark brown skin, much darker than your own. You play with your two friends until the low sun fills the room with a thick red light. You leave your host and walk along the street. Your other friend prods you in the ribs and holds his nose mockingly. He tells you that your friend is an Untouchable. You remember that your mother once used the same word to describe you, but you keep this a secret. You feel like sitting on one of the benches by the cathedral, but they are all taken. You do not feel like sitting on the grass – you can see tombstones and that would be like sitting on the dead. You keep walking along the wide pavement, around the cathedral, the dead, the grass and the people in the sunshine.

The problem of race becomes clearer when you go to secondary school. Everybody hates everybody. The Indians hate the Pakistanis, together they hate the blacks, the West Indians hate the Africans, they all hate the whites, the others get hated in equal measure, the whites hate in return. As you grow older you see the hatred within your own community: divided by caste, social standing, city of origin. Your father comes home from work and speaks of his troubles; you know who he hates. The hatred weaves itself from school to workplace, stabilizing across the different communities. At university, you begin to see it like an equation, a Newtonian law where all the energies are equal and thus cancel each other out. Occasionally there is a fluctuation, the streets inflame as if infected and someone dies.

You think little of it. Back in the shade, walking along the other side of Rackhams, you see your bus crawl along Bull Street. You start to run.

Out of breath, you reach the bus stop. A crowd of people have been waiting and they pour into the bus without any order. First you think of sitting on the bottom deck but it is already full. You follow a black woman up the stairs. When you reach the top deck, you pause and look at the available spaces. The front half is full. You feel like the bus has segregated itself, the majority of the younger black people sitting to the rear. A white man nudges you in your back, he's waiting for you to move. You walk slowly along the aisle, your eyes drifting from left to right. You see the woman whom you see on most weekday evenings. She has skin the colour of white coffee and you have never spoken to her, but your desire for her is intense. She is aware of your face and the way you look at her. You want to sit next to her but you lose your nerve. She glances up as you sit behind her, next to a thin, young black girl with narrow hips. She tuts and squeezes herself closer to the window. You could place your hand down flat between you and her if you wanted. You are sweating from the run.

You lose your virginity to a white woman. You think of her for two years and then forget. You remember her once again when you go to a hotel café and order a latte. The barista serves the drink in a tall glass with a curving metal handle. She has poured in the steamed milk first and then a double shot of espresso. Somehow they have not mixed together, and this creates a layer of brown over white. You look at your drink and remember taking your naked body off hers. You think that sex is a contrast of colours. You wonder what would happen if the two colours matched, whether they would combine never to be separated again.

The bus driver drives the bus as if it is pregnant. He speeds recklessly, careering around corners. You lean forward and hold onto the metal rail of the seat in front, you sway and try your best not to touch the girl next to you. The woman in front glances at you. You want to talk to her. The girl next to you lights a cigarette; you begin to hate her.

White people are the minority in your workplace, but of that minority, the majority are managers. You are not a manager. You work with the blacks and the browns, and the few whites with a fraternal spirit of contempt for everything you have to do. Sometimes you, and many others, are asked to leave by the back door when a client is visiting. This makes you want to hit your bosses, but you do and say nothing. You look for a proper job. You look to escape. The bus has stopped at the intersection of Hamstead Road and Villa Road. There is a long queue of traffic and the bus has overshot the traffic lights and is stuck in the middle of the crossroads, blocking the vehicles flowing along Villa Cross. You are in the heart of Handsworth. To your right is the black-and-white building of the Asian Resource Centre, on the other side the remains of the Black Cat Café. Below is the sound of car horns beating. Someone passing by bangs on the glass, you feel the pounding as a dull ache in your chest. The girl continues to smoke. You see her face reflected through the smoke drifting across the glass. For a second your memories seem as noxious as they are intoxicating. You stop thinking about the past and focus on this girl sitting next to you.

Several people, including the beautiful woman, are annoyed by the smoke, but nobody dares speak. The girl flicks some ash, it lands on your right trouser leg. You explode. You shout and tell her to put out the cigarette. The girl sucks air through her teeth and drops the cigarette to the ash-coloured floor, smothering it with her shoe. She gets up and off the bus. You, and everyone else, are relieved. You move along the seat to sit by the window. As you move you catch the eye of the beautiful white-coffee-coloured woman. This time she turns her head to look at you completely. She has brown frizzy hair, large brown eyes and a beauty spot above her lip. You know this already since you have observed her features many times. This time you feel vindicated. She is sitting next to the white man who nudged you. She smiles, thanks you and asks for your name; you give it to her without hesitation. She tells you hers and then glances forward – you know her stop is next. You want to get off with her, but you must not follow her. She stands up and gives you a wave, you say 'goodbye' and her name once more. The white man moves aside and she leaves. She is taller than you. She looks back at you as she walks down the stairs.

The bus races on and you focus on whatever the driver is pursuing. The bus becomes lighter every stop, each delivery quicker than the last. You are alone at the back where the smell of the cigarette lingers. You look at your hands and press the bell. It is your stop next. You zigzag down the aisle and the stairs and get off. The air outside is peppered by exhaust fumes. In this city of people, across these fractured communities, you have made something real. You have made a connection. You walk home, still hearing the echoes of your past, but knowing that you cannot hold on to them any more than you can hold on to puffs of smoke. You stop and look up at the sky. The azure is stretched thin and fading. You smile. You have made a new friend. Her name is Lisa.

Harpreet Singh

HARPREET SINGH was born in London and grew up in Birmingham. He is working on a series of novels that bounce around the lives of Punjabis in England from the 1960s to the present.

Earth Versus Spider
Harpreet Singh

Nobody will believe it but when she comes I have to be ready. Take the grubs and larvae and check the dimensions. Stuff like that. It's going to be Earth versus Spider and when it happens, and it will, at least one of us will have to save humanity with the knowledge. Who will have the knowledge?

I will have the knowledge.

Rufus my dog yaps a few times. He's shaggy and old, a mangy and lazy dog. A grey mongrel. We grew up together.

Take a look at this web. I checked and let it live; now there are a couple of bluebottles mummified and dead. Spider meat. I watch the arachnid wend her way down, tiptoeing and sliding on its silk and then it dashes a spike between their antennae, sucks their brains out and eats them. It dismembers them daintily, crunches and enjoys.

That's what it's going to be like when she comes, and she's coming soon. Humans will be strung up on the spider web like Egyptian mummies and they'll still be alive. They'll be able to see everything, but will be numb and paralysed in tightly bound sticky threads and a kind of acid spit, and they'll watch as she comes for them and sucks their brains and eats them up, snapping legs and arms like twigs. Crunched.

Each string of the web will be a foot thick, tougher than steel rope, so you can imagine what size Spider will be.

It's all about knowing the enemy. At night I lie still in bed and imagine being in the web. I lie tight and tense my muscles. It'll be like being frozen, I think. Then I open my eyes but know there could be no escape. Imagine having my brains slurped out through a spike straw by a gigantic insect from the centre of the Earth.

It makes me scared.

Makes me sad.

Makes me mad.

So I decided the best thing is not to get spun. That's why I have to watch, and learn. That's how I can survive. What people have to ask themselves is, 'Do I want to survive?'

Guns and bombs won't be any match for Spider because her skin is armour-plated and anyway she just spins stuff and spurts poison and her eight legs would trample on everything and everyone. And if she has to escape to protect herself she can just burrow back underground again. In nine minutes she would be three miles into the Earth's inner core. Can you imagine the rumbling? Tectonic plates in Turkey and Japan would get mashed up. Expect a tsunami to hit Okinawa. What can you do against Spider? I have to use my brain. Watch and learn.

I stroke Rufus when I need to think. I'm doing it now.

On the fourteenth of December in the year 2007, at 15.37, Spider will emerge from underneath the Houses of Parliament and start trashing up the place. I told my father and he ignored me. But I checked with Nostradamus and there's something there. Some stuff about an eight-legged beast eating the Crown of Albion. London is history. Two million dead within the first six hours. Can you imagine that kind of fury? What do you think we can do about it?

*

She's been hatching for so long and isn't going to hold back. But then Spider will calm down for a while. Her babies will be brewing inside her belly but she'll go mad if you try to test her. Trust me. Television cameras will record the moment because they'll be interviewing people outside Parliament and things will go crazy. Big Ben will crumble and there'll be screaming, and the pictures will go dead because everyone within a mile radius is toast in the first spurt of venom and madness. We'll see it emerge, about sixty seconds of shaky pictures, and then the screen will go blank. It'll be watched in horror around the world. The news will flash; the terror will begin.

But they won't understand. America's no good. Spider's been living in the core of the Earth for 65,000 years, so what do you reckon a nuke's going to do? She has lava for blood. She's got eight eyes, can see everything and everyone. If one of her legs gets chopped off it'll grow back. Spider is just one but I estimate we'll have about six days before the progeny start dropping out of her gaping womb with gunk and everything. Then it's all over. They'll have super venom. Six days till the end of the world.

Anyway, so my mum calls me in for dinner and I see the spider freeze and pause on the web. It jiggles around, like to get a better view of something. So I freeze too. Rufus pauses suddenly as well and stops wagging his tail. He looks at me to see what's going on. That's when it comes to me. It froze when it heard my mum's voice. And that's when I discovered what Spider's tactics are.

I check in the *Encyclopaedia Britannica*. Dad got it cheap from the man who owns the kennels. I read each line under my breath as Rufus squats by my ankle and looks up at me:

Spiders have eight legs and two main body parts: the prosoma, or cephalothorax, and the opisthosoma, or abdomen. They are abundant worldwide except in Antarctica and occur at elevations from sea level to 5000 metres (16,000 feet). Some 30,000 species have been described. All are terrestrial animals and range in body length from less than one millimetre to about 90 millimetres: THEY ARE PREDATORY *– mostly on insects.*

All of us as crushable and eatable as a spindly insect. All of us potential arachnid meat. Not human. Not man or woman or child with feelings and emotions and loved ones and memories. Just a piece of meat, the same as a fly or cockroach.

How many of them teeming in wait all over the globe? God help us please. Thirty thousand species. How many billions gnawing and spinning in anticipation of our geno-cide? Not billions – there must be trillions. And there's no escaping them on land. Even in the Himalayas at 16,000 feet they'll be there. Everyone on Earth will be close to one, hiding, watching, listening, learning. Pretending to be just doing their thing. But in reality sending signals and transmitting information back to Spider in the Earth's core. These are her tactics. They are spies. Her eyes. Her bugs.

I look over my shoulder. Imagine them in the corner of that room. In my bathroom. Under the skirting board. Be-neath my computer. That web in the corner? They can hear our conversations from wherever. In the garden. In your car. In Canada and India and Brazil. It's all getting relayed back. I'm scared and numb to think of us all oblivious, with just me aware. Humankind thought spiders were living their lives, spinning their webs and munching on flies. We never dared to imagine the horror and evil they will bring.

So it froze when it heard Mum's voice. Now Spider knows where I live, who my mum is, what time we eat dinner, what time Dad comes home, when Rufus sleeps, walks, eats and shits. This crafty fly-eater will have transmitted all our information. But if I kill this spider-spy now, she will know I know. It's a game of bluff and counter-bluff. It's a shady world of psychological duelling. So I walk indoors, all casual like, as if I didn't notice him freeze. Let Spider think I'm oblivious. Rufus follows me.

Now, if the worst comes to the worst we'll have to make our way to Antarctica. There aren't any spiders there so the future of mankind may well be Eskimo. We could at least scheme there without being suspected. It's one of her fatal flaws. Everything has a weakness, you see. You just have to discover what it is and exploit it. Because then her weakness becomes your strength.

I sit there at the dinner table eating my fish fingers really slow. I try and act normal. Mum and Dad are asking my brothers and sisters about their day and what they did at school. I'm trying to fit some peas and fish finger on my fork.

Then Dad asks me, 'How was your day, Spiderman?'

I flinch. Try to act calm. If I tell them I'll start a panic. Sort out the plan first, then tell them. I don't want to cause a stampede. Peas fall off my fork and bounce up and down on the plate.

They think I'm going through this phase where I'm interested in spiders and stuff, like I'm a kid who'll be collecting books on something else next month. Got about a hundred books on spiders from the library, been printing out stuff from the Internet.

So I just calmly cut off another piece of fish finger, and say, 'Fine, Dad. Had a good day. Did some more research. Did you know that the Black Widow is also known as the Red Hourglass because of the markings on its body?'

He gets bored and sarcastic. 'Oh really, how fascinating, so interesting . . .'

And he looks away. Everyone laughs. Sometimes I think it wouldn't be so bad if Spider got him while the rest of my family escaped. I ask Mum to pass the ketchup, and squirt some in.

For the rest of the meal I try hard not to show my fears. I keep picturing the Seven Wonders of the World destroyed. Spider's going to ruin them all. The Statue of Liberty all wrapped up in a web. The Taj Mahal cracked apart and smouldering. The Sphinx and Pyramids crushed. The Eiffel Tower in a chrysalis. I feel sad because I would have liked to see those things. I wouldn't have minded London getting wasted; I hate cockneys. But I always wanted to see New York and the Eiffel Tower. I munch on a fish finger and feel better. Fish fingers always make me feel better.

I go up to my room and lie on my bed. Time is running out. One line runs through my brain: *Spider is coming for you.*

Rufus joins me and squats in the corner. I call him over and he sits on my stomach. I stroke him to get my mind to work.

Then I try the Internet.

I log on and type 'Spider: End of the World: Help!' into the search engine and spend the next few hours clicking on links. There must be others like me who know the truth out there, who are trying to make contact with those that know. But every link leads me to a morass of arachnid details and irrelevancies and leaves me frustrated and close to defeat.

Three months ago I went to the doctor and saw a spider's web in the corner of the waiting-room ceiling. Things collided in my mind. He was working for the beast. That's why he gave me these pills to eat to make me hallucinate.

I've been feeding them to Rufus and flushing them down the toilet so my family thinks I'm still taking the medicine. But she's crafty. She infiltrated Dr Singh's brain and gave him telepathic instructions. Tried to disable me by pretending I need potions to make me see the truth, pretending I had an ailment in between my ears. But I'm free from the deceivers. The day is coming. I will stand alone in history.

I decide that I should provoke Spider. I'll get some poison and start killing every spy in the house. She'll be forced to make the next move, knowing I'm onto her plan. I wait for everyone to go to sleep, then go into the back garden and destroy the web of the money spider that thought he knew me. And that's just the start. It's going to be genocide around here. An arachnid pogrom.

I look in the fridge. Two fish fingers left over from dinner. I eat one as I walk upstairs. As I enter the room, Rufus has a guilty look on his face. I chuck him a fish finger, which he catches in his mouth, and I lie down to look at my atlas to check how far it is to Antarctica.

I become aware of a strange sensation, as though I'm being stared at. Whenever I turn around, Rufus looks away sneakily and pretends to be doing something else. This happens a few times.

Eventually, I notice that the computer is switched on although the monitor is turned off. I stand and flick the switch. The screen has the sent message page of an email account.

It is then that I see the paw marks on the mouse and keyboard. I press Back on the toolbar and read this email:

To: CanineIntelligenceService@hotmail.com
Re: Project Puppy
From: Rufus the Defecator

Dear Comrade
All modalities accepted. Tertiary plan in place. Give
a dog a bone. Proceed to final solution.
-R-

It grows in me, slowly, heartbeat-punching slow, fast, fast, faster, now an accelerated sense of horror and pitiful under-standing as things fall into place, every petty moment and mistake I've made these past few months. Images come to mind, memories of how Rufus has conveniently been present at times when I've begun to understand the threat man-kind was facing, always watching, observing, leading me here, influencing me there . . .

Eventually I hold my stomach and look at the mongrel.

He is staring straight at me, baring drooling fangs in a satanic Hades grin. Horror numbs down my face like slowly dripping candle wax and, my throat dry, I can only say, 'You?'

Rufus goes crazy and starts jumping about and barking.

'Yes! Yes! Me! You fool! You blind fool! It's not Earth versus Spider! It's Earth versus Dog! EARTH VERSUS DOG!'

It isn't strange that he speaks to me in English, any more than it's strange for a boy in his death throes to contem-plate the inexplicable fact that soon he will no longer exist. All that's left is resignation. Rufus – you dirty traitor, you wretched, evil son of a bitch.

'Ras the Retromingent is coming! The Equalizing Bitch! The Doberman Destroyer! And there's nothing you can do about it because she's coming tonight! We knew only you could stand in our way so I have shepherded you all your life to this point! Did you really think those pathetic insects could challenge you? The age of *Homo sapiens* will soon be at an end. You failed. We'll see who takes who for a walk soon!'

I know that at this moment my family are standing outside the door and are removing their human masks to reveal their true grinning dog heads underneath. Growling, with their teeth bared and eyes red, rabies salivating. Yes, I know my teachers at school and Dr Singh and all the others are shedding their disguises now too. I see the world collapse in the face of their fury, contempt and rage, as the dogs slaughter us and destroy our civilization, rip us apart between their teeth, packs of dogs howling and hounding, chasing us to eat our meat and chew on our splintered bones. I have failed. I scream as a deceived boy who has seen his loyal best friend bite out his heart, and cock his leg and piss on the wound screams – a fur-curdling scream – then all I can say is:

'No!'

'Yes!'

'NO!'

'YESSS!'

'NOOOOO!'

'Woof! I mean, YES! Prepare to be domesticated!'

It is at this moment that all light in my eyes deletes into black crystals and I hold a scream in my throat.

I hold it because there's no point in screaming in this world any more, because all that will count is the growl and bark of our coming slave masters, the *grrrr* and roar of the new barbarians.

Simran Kaur in Great Barr

Harpreet Singh

I'd been writing short stories for almost a year when one day my English teacher, Mrs Smith, told me to stay behind after class for a few minutes.

'I have read your last two stories, Simran, and I have to say they are good. Nicely poised and structured. Some excellent use of language and imagery. But just one thing troubles me.'

Mrs Smith was my mentor. At least, she wanted to be. She had coaxed me and taken a special interest in my writing after catching me reading *The Prime of Miss Jean Brodie* behind the bike sheds one afternoon. I was blowing bubbles, seeking some quiet during the lunch break. She was on truancy duty, checking up on which Indian youth were at the daytime bhangra disco in town instead of school.

'You see, Simran, you're a seventeen-year-old Sikh girl living in Birmingham in the year 1991, but you keep writing about nineteenth-century upper-class ladies in country houses and mansions falling in love with unsuitable men. Now, I love Jane Austen as much as you do, but I'm telling you this because I value your writing so much. I wouldn't say it if you had no talent. It is high time that the authentic voice of the Indian experience in Britain was heard.'

I panicked. 'But I don't have any stories to tell, Miss. My life is so boring. I don't feel very authentic. My life . . .

it's just nothing. Just getting up and going to school and that's it, really.'

'Yes, Simran. And these are the things you need to tell the world. About the stifling constriction of your life. The people that surround you. The dreams, hopes and aspirations of your community. God knows I've been living in Birmingham for long enough and we need a strong authentic Indian voice to protest against the racism of white society and the oppression that you face at home every day.'

I felt confused. 'But Miss, I don't think I've ever had racism or oppression.'

'Don't be silly, Simran. Of course you have, you just haven't noticed it.' She sighed. 'You poor girl. Brainwashed and conditioned to be blind to your own subjugation. Now, this is what you will do. Keep a diary. Write in it your observations of your life and family. Basically, all the things happening in the Indian community that you live and breathe in. The cruelty of your men, how you are torn between two worlds, you know, all the superstitious religiosity of your people, that kind of thing.'

I had never thought of myself as being apart from the average before. I was just me. As normal as the trees and lampposts that lined our street. Why did I have to ponder my existence any more than they had to?

'Naipaul. Selvon. Narayan. Why can they write about Indian lives and you cannot?'

I suspected it was a trick question. 'Umm. I dunno. Because they're so clever. And they know and write about real places, not boring shitty Birmingham. Oh, sorry.'

'It's okay, Simran. I understand your frustration. What is one swear-word in the face of so much real profanity in your life? Carry on.'

'They – well, I don't really know why I can't write like them, Miss.'

'Exactly. Because you have been brainwashed by the cultural imperialism of this society, and the patriarchy of your own people, to place no value on your own experiences. Brainwashed to think that literature can only be about middle-class and upper-class white people having headaches over their doomed love affairs. It's a self-esteem problem, Simran.'

It certainly made sense to me, although I wasn't aware that my brain had been so comprehensively washed without my permission.

'Once you start making observations in your diary, stories will suggest themselves to you. And finally you will be able to make a protest against the racism and gender oppression that destroys so many Indian girls' lives. And that may destroy yours too, one day. It's so tragic.'

I shook my head at the tragedy of it all.

'Simran, I wasted whatever talent I had, never got published. But in you I can see . . .'

I made my excuses hastily and left. I always felt uncomfortable with the self-pitying introspection she invariably ended her advice with. My friends said she was a lesbian who was after my thighs, not my mind.

Her encouragement was precious to me, though, and in a way I loved her for it.

I bought a new writing pad on the way home and settled to keep a diary. Mrs Smith had rattled a truth that had been teasing at me for some months. It was time to stop writing about white people, as though they were the only ones who had lives of interest and gravity.

For the next few weeks I made banal observations about my daily life in the diary. I tried to include my whole family in it. I told of how my father came home from work and fell asleep on the sofa straight away. He was working before dawn and beyond dusk, establishing a building supplies business he had set up with some redundancy money from the smelting factory he'd worked in since coming to England in the 1960s. I wrote about my baby brother Tappan and his cute exploits, and about how my mother offered to buy me contact lenses so I could be more confident about myself.

One evening, as we sat in the lounge drinking tea, she said, 'It's because of these books she's reading all the time. Now, reading is a good thing if it makes you clever but not if it makes you go blind. No point being clever and blind.'

My sister Preeti was filing her nails and chewing gum. She was nineteen and studying to be a beautician at Handsworth College. This was my mother's occupation too, and it was their dream to open a beauty salon together.

Preeti said, 'It's true, Mum, she just reads all the time and doesn't even let me practise on her hair and face. Those books just make her look so boring. I'm embarrassed to be seen with her, I swear.'

My father was pretending to be snoozing and said, 'Shut up, both of you. Always criticizing about this and that. Girl here is a genius and all you're worried about is your fingernails and what lipstick to wear.'

He opened one eye and laughed at Preeti's new perm. She scowled at him and stomped upstairs.

Tappan climbed on top of me and yanked my nose. I told him off.

Mum looked up from the cardigan she was knitting and said, 'I don't believe it. The quiet one has spoken. Don't do this because I will almost have a heart attack with the shock. I will go to the gurdwara tomorrow and thank God for the few words you just gave us.'

Dad laughed. They always complained about my silences, and often observed me observing others.

I went to sleep that night without making an entry in my

diary, and some days later I threw it into the dustbin by the shops at the bottom of our road. My admissions had become increasingly dark. After being pestered by Preeti one night I had written:

My sister is such a slag. If she doesn't stop annoying me I'm telling everyone about Dippa and Stan and all her boyfriends.

Another day my only insight was:

Mum and Dad went to Coventry. Ate some chicken legs. Had a bath. Went to sleep.

I avoided Mrs Smith, and fell into an apathy about writing and reading. I couldn't discern any stories or meaning in the lives that surrounded and elided mine. There was blankness within and without me and my mentor sensed my inability to see. We lapsed into the normal relationship between student and teacher.

My life trundled forward unremarkably until Mangal and Neeta moved into the house behind us at the beginning of March.

By protocol we should have called them Aunty and Uncle because they were our parents' best friends, but they insisted we call them by their first names. Mangal and Dad were like brothers. They grew up together in our village back in India. We all helped them to unpack their belongings from the removal van which had arrived from Smethwick.

That evening they ate dinner with us. I didn't know why they had moved to Great Barr, away from their family, so when Mangal declaimed the perfidy of his brothers it was a revelation to me. Some dispute between them had escalated to such high proportions of insult that it forced them to seek refuge with us.

'I told him. I told him but he would not let it lie. Then she talks all about Neeta behind her back, saying she's fat, and the reason we can't have children is because she is so fat.'

I was transfixed by a trace of gravy sliding down his chin. With melodramatic incredulity, he asked us if we thought she was fat. Neeta was slightly plump, but certainly not obese. I could feel embarrassment and tension shaving off in sparks from Neeta as she anticipated a response.

Dad said, 'Not as fat as you.'

Mangal shyly touched his potbelly and tried to stare sternly at his wife when she sniggered at this response. I wanted to stifle my laugh too but couldn't, and this brought me to my father's attention. He was a little drunk. Whenever Mangal came round they brought the whisky bottle out.

We finished dinner and I sat in silence for the rest of the evening, just watching and listening to my family.

That night before I went to sleep I started another diary and scrawled:

Mangal and Neeta are our neighbours now. Mangal fights with his brothers. Neeta cannot have babies. That's why she's always holding Tappan.

Then in capital letters and underlined I wrote:

<u>MUST SPEAK MORE</u>
<u>BE MORE ACTIVE</u>
<u>FIND YOURSELF</u>

We all helped to decorate their house. After work Dad would spend his evenings there while Neeta lounged with us and cooked dinner. One evening she looked so glum. She used to work in the warehouse that Mangal's brother owned in Hockley, and would occasionally drive a forklift when staff was short.

'I have the strong arms to turn the wheel, see.' She rolled up her sleeve and showed us the impressive girth of her forearms. Then she looked down and started sobbing, and recounted how she felt isolated at home and so foolish without a job, especially without children to look after and with the pressure of estrangement from their family.

Mum put down the spoon she was stirring the food with and said, 'Neeta, I've had enough of this moaning from you. We're going to the job centre tomorrow and we're not leaving until they give you some work. Who can deny you work? Who dares to? Look at your arms! All you have to do is roll up the sleeve and show them your strong muscles and tell them that you can drive tanks and things. Stop the crying. Stop sitting at home all day moping.'

At this moment Mangal walked in and shouted at Neeta for some offence she'd committed, and then stormed out again to return to their house with a hacksaw from the tool-box Dad stored on the shelf next to the washing machine.

Preeti said, 'That wasn't very nice.'

Neeta's face blushed with despair and persecution. She rubbed her eyes and motioned for us to come near her. 'It's not my fault that we have no babies. I'm ready to make them. It's him.'

Preeti, Mum and I looked at each other conspiratorially. Neeta nodded her head. 'I'm all woman and a baby-maker. But he, it's him that can't do his job . . . Then he comes in and shouts at me. You know how many times we've tried . . .'

Mum glanced at me, a little uncomfortable that I'd heard this. Preeti put her arms around Neeta and said, 'Aunty, I'm taking you to college tomorrow after job centre, and we're going to get your hair cut nice like Mum's. You know Jaswinder is training to be hairdresser? Then I'm going to make you up, because you're all woman, working and correct.'

That night my diary entry ran:

Neeta is all woman but Mangal can't give her babies. His grapes are seedless. Mum and Preeti are going to make her look nice and feel good though.

I put the diary away and got into bed, but something was stirring in my cerebrum. I switched on the light, recovered my journal and wrote:

I think Neeta feels emptiness, because she has no babies and no job. No friends or family except us. No family after arguments in Smethwick. Mangal's brothers kicked him out. We are their only hope.

Two weeks later Neeta was called for an interview as a trainee bus driver with West Midlands Transport. After six weeks' training she passed her test and was assigned to the number 17 route from West Bromwich to Dudley, driving a red single-decker seven hours a day.

We had a sense of the struggle that came with this. Mangal had been demoted at work and the tension and silences between him and his wife were apparent each time they stepped inside our house.

Mangal grumbled one evening when he was drinking with Dad. 'My wife as a bus driver . . . too much shame if my brothers see this.'

Dad gave his wisdom. 'Mangal, you should hush about this thing. At the speed you're going at soon your wife will be earning more than you. It is a good thing that she is making a living.'

Mangal was indignant and said, 'She looks like a truck anyway.'

But this was not true.

Preeti and Mum had refined her, giving her a fashionable haircut, waxing her facial hair and advising her as to the best make-up to emphasize her features. Preeti had found a pliant muse and model for her beautifying, and after work Neeta would come straight to our house and regale us with tales from the day's run. She had bought a trendy blue denim jacket and wore it over her salwar kameez and wore a pair of white Adidas trainers. This became her uniform, and she fast became a joy to the passengers on her route – especially the old Indians, with whom she would banter in Punjabi and drop off and pick up directly outside the gurdwara in Oldbury, even though there wasn't a bus stop there.

One Saturday Preeti and I spent the whole afternoon riding beside her in the bus, just chatting and enjoying the day out. All the passengers called her by her first name, and some children even bought chocolate and sweets for her, which she shared with us afterwards.

That evening Mangal didn't come over to the house.

Mum said, 'Is he hungry? Maybe we should take him some food over.'

Neeta replied with irritation, 'Does Mangal ever stay hungry? Let him be.'

Everyone made jokes about him and let him be.

We saw less of Mangal as the year slouched towards summer.

One day in July Dad came home late from the pub and told us that Mangal had had to take a pay cut in a redundancy sweep at his firm in order to keep his job.

Granduncle said, 'Just tell Neeta to come over here now to spare the poor girl his moans tonight then.'

He'd taken to travelling with her one day a week in the morning, getting dropped off at the gurdwara, where he'd spend all day making new friends and relaxing until she collected him in the afternoon.

'And another thing. Isn't it the truth that when a man

loses money, he should buy less food and become less fat. But in Mangal's case the opposite happens. It is strange.'

Everybody laughed again at Mangal's expense. We were all in high spirits that night because the next day Neeta was due to appear on the local evening news. West Midlands Transport had promoted her as a public relations representative: the only female Indian bus driver in the region and an example of their commitment to equal opportunities and good race relations.

We all sat in febrile excitement before the TV the following evening. I held my finger over the record button on our chunky VCR. Neeta was grinning, holding Mum and Preeti's hands. My sister had given her a full beauty treatment on the morning of the interview. Mangal was sat at the back, pretending to be asleep. He was roused to say, 'Oh. What's all the hype? It's no big thing. Just wake me up when it starts.'

If any of us praised his wife or expressed our affection for her during his feigned slumber, he snored so loudly it almost drowned all thought, let alone speech. He quietened down when we changed the topic.

Granduncle waddled in and motioned at Mangal with rude exasperation, then sat beside Neeta.

Dad said, 'Press it now!'

I released the record button and silence hugged us all. The previous item, about an eccentric water dowser from Staffordshire, had just ended. The newsreader, a middle-aged white man wearing a wig and a smug, grey polyester suit, looked straight into the camera and began speaking.

'Now, we all know about the fantastic contribution made to the West Midlands by our Indian community. But an amazing Birmingham woman is breaking new ground. Emily Rozenburg reports.'

There followed a two-minute feature on how Neeta had

succeeded in becoming the most popular bus driver on her route, and how she represented the true pioneering spirit of West Midlands Indian women, and the righteous egalitarianism of the bus company.

'Repressed? Shy? Lazy? Stay-at-home? Baby factories? Is that what you think of Indian women? Well, think again . . .'

We all looked at Neeta and she blushed.

'Neeta Kaur, a 38-year-old former housewife from Great Barr, is breaking stereotypes the way that bus drivers on the number 17 route used to break speed limits . . .'

I got a jerky thrill when I saw Neeta onscreen, with her new bouncy curly hairstyle and gold wedding jewellery glistening in the sunshine. I turned between the real Neeta and TV Neeta in amazement, and she opened her eyes wide at me, sharing the excitement of our moment.

In the report she was grinning whenever she appeared in front of the camera.

The real Neeta said, 'They told me to be serious, but I couldn't stop smiling, I was so happy.'

The reporter asked her how it felt to be the only Indian woman bus driver in the Midlands.

'Oh yeah, it feels good you know, I'm very happy, ha-haha, I love my job, yes. I like to thank my husband, who inspire me to be a bus driver.'

We all turned to look at Mangal. He gave an embarrassed shrug, his lips locked in a struggle to suppress an insurgent smile.

'It's good, shows that Indian woman can do anything as long as she loves God, and ummm, I hope lots of Punjabi girls watching this now can be inspire, you know, to become the bus driver one day. They can do anything they want, ummm, bus driver, doctor, have their own clothes shop, you know, selling the saris. I hope lots of Indian girls become bus drivers too.' She giggled.

There then followed a series of vox pops with passengers on the bus.

An elderly white woman said, 'Oooh she's lovely. I think she's lovely. She even speaks English. If she wasn't married I'd take her home to meet my son, Nigel. He's forty-five and not married yet. Can you imagine?'

A wrinkly, white-bearded Indian man said something incomprehensible in heavily accented pidgin English, then threw his head back and burst out laughing.

A plump Jamaican girl said shyly, 'She beat up the bullies that used to beat me up on the way home from school. Now they don't bully me no more.'

There were some shots of Neeta walking out of the driver's cabin, supposedly naturally, but she didn't stop smiling into the camera. The report ended with: 'So don't be surprised if you find community relations running smoothly, and on time, on the number 17 route to Dudley. Emily Rozenburg, *Midlands Tonight*.'

The camera cut to the newsreader, who was shuffling his papers. He gave a cheeky smile and said, 'Great stuff. Typical, though. You wait ages for a female Indian bus driver to come along, and there'll probably be another three coming soon, right behind her.'

The blonde weathergirl to his right chortled at his joke. Dad swore at him.

We rewound the tape and watched it fourteen times in a row, except for Mangal, who excused himself, claiming tiredness and stomach ache.

That evening I wrote reams in my diary. The next day I approached Mrs Smith during lunch break to tell her that I was keeping my journal again, just as she'd advised me to.

'That's excellent, Simran. I hope you are collecting lots of good material. When can I hope to see some your new stories?'

'Ummm. Maybe next term, Miss. After the summer holidays.'

'I look forward to it, I really do. Still reading Jane Austen, eh? Your stories, are they all about you and your life? Your curries and saris and chutney and exotic fruits? We want to read the truth about your reality, Simran, about how the life of India exists like magical realism on the streets of Birmingham. Are you writing about your people?'

'Well, yeah. But I was thinking of putting some of your white people into them too.'

'Well, you don't know how excited I am by it. Look, take this home and read it in your spare time.' She handed me a copy of Sam Selvon's *A Brighter Sun*.

I thanked her idly and nodded my head as she gave me another lecture about being true to myself. But I wasn't sure what was my self that I had to be true to. And I wondered why she was so interested in it anyway. When she told me all those stereotype things I wanted to punch her on the nose and tell her to mind her own business.

As vivid as some events in my life seemed, I felt deflated at the thought of fashioning fiction from the drabness of the streets and routines that merged to form my existence.

After my exams I determined to spend the summer holidays reading and doing little else. Halfway through *To Kill a Mockingbird* I realized my eyesight was faltering again, and Dad took me to the opticians for a new prescription. Mum banned me from reading for more than an hour a day, fearful of myopia, but I cheated her in snatched corners of the long summer, happy and bloated with relaxation. *A Brighter Sun* sat unread in my bedroom, and often I would spend the entire day riding in Neeta's bus with Tappan, keeping her company, and reading the over-due copy of *Huckleberry Finn* that I owed to Handsworth Library.

Once, as we bounced along a potholed road near Tipton, I imagined my little brother as poor orphan Oliver Twist, and it almost brought me to tears, until he pulled my hair and I had to clean snot from his hay-feverish nose. Another time I just browsed through *Emma* in an afternoon, referring back to one of my favourite-ever lines: *One has no great hopes from Birmingham. I always say there is something direful in the sound.*

I memorized this sentence, scrawled it over my schoolbook covers, and read it again and again on that bus as we trawled through the Black Country. I checked the publication date: 1812. It left me even more in awe of Jane Austen's prescience and wisdom, and amazed that at least she knew the name of the place in which I floated, the direful nothingness of Simran Kaur in Great Barr.

Diwali came upon us quickly that year, and I still hadn't written any stories. Mangal wanted us to spend the holy day with him, because it was the first Diwali in their new house.

'I bought the whole batch of Monee's fireworks from last year. Thousands of them. It's going to be the biggest explosion ever. We'll invite loads of people, eh? Or no, better still, just have immediate family, just the two of us, nice and cosy together, little bonfire, some fireworks, Tappan will love this, eh?'

Preeti and I glanced at each other and Mum nudged at Dad. He told him our plans.

'Actually, brother, we are all thinking of going to Handsworth Park on Diwali after gurdwara. Council is putting on a show. Fireworks, bhangra.'

Preeti said, 'Apna Sangeet is going to be there.'

'Yeah, all the top bands, and a massive bonfire, fireworks, everything. It's going to be good. Uncle is going too, aren't you, Uncle?'

'Oh yes. It's going to be good.' He said this without looking up from that week's copy of the Punjabi newspaper. 'And I want little Tappan to see all the rumpus and fun. Come along too.'

Neeta put down her coffee cup and said, 'Oh yes, let's go to the park too. There's going to be thousands there.'

There was a pause, a shuffle, then Mangal stood up and said, 'I'm sick of all of you making me cry. Now I want to cry because everything I say you say no to and you make a fool of me and laugh. Well, you can go to the park. I'm having fireworks at home and that's it. And when you're standing in Handsworth Park look to the hill because my fireworks are going to be bigger than any Council fireworks. Going to a Council Diwali party. Organized by whitey! What does whitey know about Diwali? And you . . .' He pointed at Neeta. 'You make up your mind who you are with, never listening to me any more. When my fireworks go off they'll think the Russians have launched an attack. And you still want to do your own thing. I'm sick of being made a fool of. You all think I'm a fat idiot too, so you can all jump in the well. Goodnight.'

He crashed out of the door and we heard him running around the corner.

Neeta stood up slowly and said apologetically, 'When I became top driver, it was very hard for him. Maybe I should just give it up and look after him.'

She followed him home. Through the cotton net curtains of our back window I saw her shoulders slumped and her face gasping in sorrow down at her feet as she walked along the suddenly sad pavement.

Dad sighed and said, 'This is what happens when a man cannot make a baby. He becomes a baby himself.'

For the two weeks running up to Diwali Mangal barricaded himself into his house and didn't come to see us once. Gradually we saw a huge bonfire take shape in his back garden. It towered above the fence. Granduncle said, 'I hope he's not planning to make Neeta do the suttee.'

I spied him one evening, loading the back shed with cartons of fireworks, and I reported to Dad. He sucked his teeth. 'He's acting too strange. No wonder his brothers have kicked him out. Let's just hope he keeps a bucket of water next to him. I don't care any more. Just let him do his own thing. Big baby.'

The day before Diwali Neeta sneaked in to see us. 'I think he's gone mad. All he does is talk about his fireworks lighting up the sky, and how if nobody comes to his Diwali party you aren't his friends any more. I don't know what to do.'

'Just stay with him, Neeta. I'm not spending Diwali with a big sulking donkey like him. Afterwards I will give him some slaps and tell him to behave himself.'

I scribbled some words about Mangal's behaviour in my diary, and started reviewing my entries to make sense of the last few months. I imagined myself into the body of a lazy girl from the village back in India, observing the running and fuss of little lives.

Handsworth Park was transformed into a Punjabi funfair on Diwali day. We lit candles at the gurdwara, then we walked with the crowds and made it in time to see the bonfire being sparked into blaze. Preeti flirted with her many boyfriends and Tappan bounced around excitedly. I stood with some friends. The cold air made our breath freeze and we listened to the bands play. Then the fireworks came and gave me a stiff neck as I looked up to see them disperse in rippling booms above our heads. We all oohed and aahed – their exploding fractals and spectrums made us happy to be together. I held my brother's hand. My father and mother rested their palms on my shoulders.

Just as Dad pulled the family together to get some food, Neeta came bounding up to us. Mum, Preeti, Tappan and I hugged her. We said as one, 'We missed you!'

Neeta had to shout over the noise of the music and the rides and the sparklers that Tappan waved in the air. 'I've had enough! I've been looking for you all for the last hour, there are too many people here! I've had enough. The crybaby told me to get out of his house so I said, "Forget this. I'm leaving this house. I wanted to give birth to a baby, not marry one." I brought the bus after work too, so we can fit everyone back!'

I was a little high in my head. We danced bhangra for the rest of the evening and when it was time to leave we walked over to the number 17 parked at the top of Grove Lane. Dad had rounded up a bunch of his friends and people who lived on the route to Great Barr. The bus filled up and we moved off, the clutch scraping and horn tooting. Somebody produced some bottles of whisky, and women started singing. The windows steamed up. As we approached Great Barr beyond Handsworth Wood we could see the houses into which Indians had slowly seeped with greater prosperity in these nominally white suburbs. At random points porches and doorways were lit up with candles in the October night, proclaiming the triumph of light over darkness. Neeta dropped a few people off, but by the time we reached the top of our hill, around twelve of Dad's friends and their families came into our house for a party.

Mum started making pakoras and Dad began pouring drinks for the men. Tappan was in a state of blind excitement, wrestling and playing with the children. Preeti went around asking the ladies about their beauty regimes. When I walked into the kitchen I saw Neeta and Mum sneakily drinking a glass of sherry each. They laughed when they saw me.

Mum said, 'Hurry round and fetch Mangal. Just tell him to come and join the party.'

I ran and knocked on the door. There was no reply. I knocked again. When I got back and told them Neeta said, 'He's just sulking. Let him sulk.'

About an hour later we heard a big explosion.

We watched from the rear windows as fireworks flew off at random, bouncing off the walls and fences of our semi-detached houses. The bonfire erupted into heavy flames, licking the sky in a starved orange frenzy. There were dozens of simultaneous eruptions and the cracking, whistling pyrotechnical rainbow squall sounded, just as Mangal had promised, as though the Russians had launched the big mushrooms onto Brum.

A rocket flew over our house with a whizz and clash. Neeta held her head in her hands. Granduncle giggled to himself. All the children jumped up and down to watch the display, chirping in Brummie yam-yam, like chimpanzees from Dudley Zoo being fed after a famine.

I ran upstairs and watched as the fireworks ignited and launched out of control, and eventually saw Mangal's silhouette duck as a Catherine Wheel span towards him, missing his head by a foot. He got up and ran indoors just as the flames of the bonfire caught the wooden fence that divided our gardens.

I wished my imagination could create irradiated tints, light, styles and cartwheels like those I was seeing. It seemed as if these coloured sparks were flying off from the inside of our heads. The squeals sounded like our craziness. It was demented like the frenzy of our lives. Beautiful and terrifying, like us, idiotic and true, a thousand manic explosions. It made sense to me. Diwali in Great Barr, all the stars, smoke, blue-green-red-orange-yellow-bang-crack-snap-whistle-boom-zoom.

Within thirty minutes the fire brigade had drowned the pyro with foam, and water dripped from the walls of our houses and sheds. Preeti put some film in the camera and took photos of us with the firemen as we served them tea. They were very friendly and understanding. Neighbours gawped and the air stayed musky with the taste of smoke. I looked at Mangal sitting in his garden with Neeta. His face was black with soot, and he grinned at me cheekily, with sharp red gums and a gap where his front teeth should have been.

Later, when everyone else was sleeping, I heard him and Dad talking downstairs, and I slipped out of bed. I lay on the landing at the head of the staircase, the carpet a fuzzy bulge on my cheek, and listened to their conversation. I could hear the jangle of ice in glasses.

'Mangal. You know we all love you, so why don't you just say what is troubling you so much instead of playing the fool?'

Mangal sighed. 'Just look at me. Just look at me. I'm a stupid old man. When I was younger I thought I would have at least one son by now. I'm a failure. What do I have? What have I got? My brothers hate me. My wife is a bus driver, she earns more than me, runs about on the television. I have to take a pay cut and bow and beg not to be sacked. What did I do wrong? And now you all hate me too. I hate this world. It's too cruel!'

I heard Dad slam down his glass and slap Mangal. It sounded like he'd hit him sharply on his bald spot.

'Ouch.'

'Now listen here. We are sick and tired of all this nonsense. We grew up together and I never had a younger brother except you. So stop this foolishness now. You stupid fat self-pitying fool. I have spent the last two weeks of my life out of my brain worrying what to do about you.'

I could feel Mangal cower as Dad continued with a stern lecture about love, friendship and the need to deny victory to introspective pity. Eventually he said, 'So you think we don't know how hard it is not to have children? It's a good thing you married such a clever girl as Neeta. For the last two months we've been going with her to the Council every week, to find out about adoption. Remember last year the little Indian baby was abandoned next to the canal in Wolverhampton? They are crying, begging for Indian people to adopt the homeless Indian children. We are going to put your name down for one and you are going to have a family. Anything to stop your whingeing. You fat bald donkey.'

There was silence, until Mangal said, 'Naah . . . Indian baby? Abandoned? Don't believe it. How could an Indian ever abandon their baby?'

'Grow up, Mangal. Open your eyes. It's happening all the time. Runaways, drug addicts, children running wild, that's the reality these days. Girls having children, then giving them away for shame. Just because you don't see these things you don't think they are happening with Indians? Brother, things are changing. Nobody cares about the old ways any more. Soon in time, a couple of generations from now, Preeti and Simran's children, all the Indians in this country will be slitting each other's throats and burning down each other's homes. Same as always. So just build yourself a family and barricade it. Because that's all you can hope for. That one or two people will love you when your days are up.'

There followed a long silence.

Then Mangal said, 'But it would be nice. Take care of a little Indian baby. Raise him up as my own. My own child!'

I sneaked to my bedroom and wrote in my diary until I fell asleep with the ballpoint in my hand. When I awoke to frosty morning sunshine it had leaked black ink over my hands, cheek and pillow. Looking in the bathroom mirror I wished it was indelible; I wanted and needed to be stained in this way.

So it was that Mangal and Neeta set the course to adopt an Indian baby.

Dad said, 'It is a good idea, especially for Mangal, whose shotgun only fires blank bullets these days.'

After a few weeks it was decided to knock down the fence separating Mangal's house from ours, so that we could have one large shared garden. We would plant vegetables and herbs on one part, to save us money and grow things together. 'To put down roots,' said Dad. We spent a whole week cutting and pulling up the grass and when we took delivery of the new turf we all got together to dig and lay.

I quickly became bored of this work though, and Dad sent me to fetch the whisky bottle to spice their tea with. He sensed I was reluctant to get my hands dirty.

I went to my bedroom and watched them all from the window.

What I saw was Mangal supping flavoured tea in the corner. Tappan building castles in the soil. Preeti turning the earth with a trowel. Mum and Neeta gossiping while they brought out snacks. I could smell our dinner simmering downstairs.

My father lay down fertilizer and watered the ground. I stared at his thick frame and wide-shouldered stance, his set neck and generous arms. I opened and closed my hands and saw the tendons flex as my fingers curled and unfurled. Those tendons were his tendons. My hands came from his.

I put on my glasses to study him more carefully. He looked up and smiled at me. I stuck my thumb up at him and he did the same in reply. Tappan spotted me aloft and fell over in his excitement at seeing me seeing him. Preeti walked over to pick him up and dust down his wool mittens and trousers. Mum and Neeta smiled at me and moved towards the kitchen.

It was so gloomy outside that the thought of them coming indoors, where we would rest together in intimacy and familiarity, warmed me. I felt a little ashamed because I had no hand or head or heart for this work that they all did: digging, building, beautifying, growing and cooking.

Instead I stretched out on my bed, closed my eyes and fell asleep. When I awoke I lay in blankness for some time, until I felt the calm of complete, unchallengeable stillness placing me at its centre. Then I sensed patterns of life spreading out and connecting somewhere on the periphery, just out of sight. I could appreciate their chatter and movement, taking shape slowly, speaking in strange accents. I closed my eyes and waited for something to begin. I saw them line up to tell me their tales, in confidence and with care, just for me and my family.

About the Editor

DEBJANI CHATTERJEE is one of Britain's best-known Asian writers, 'a poet full of wit and charm' (Andrew Motion). She grew up in India, Japan, Bangladesh, Hong Kong, Egypt and Morocco. Debjani chairs the National Association of Writers in Education and is a Royal Literary Fund Fellow. Award-winning anthologies she has edited include *Barbed Lines* and *The Redbeck Anthology of British South Asian Poetry*. Sheffield Hallam University awarded her an honorary doctorate for services to Literature.